DON'T SHOOT!

DON'T SHOOT!

Chase R's Top Ten Reasons NOT to Move to the Country

Michael J. Rosen

CANDLEWICK PRESS

CAMBRIDGE, MASSACHUSETTS

Copyright © 2002 by Michael J. Rosen

First paperback edition 2007
Originally published as *ChaseR: A Novel in E-Mails*

The Library of Congress has cataloged the hardcover edition as follows:

Rosen, Michael J.
ChaseR: a novel in e-mails / Michael J. Rosen. —1st ed.
Summary: When his parents decide to move to an old house in the country, Chase uses e-mail to his friends back in Columbus, Ohio, and to his sister in college to help him deal with cicadas, deer hunters, and other changes in his life.
ISBN 978-0-7636-1538-3 (hardcover)
[1. Country life—Fiction. 2. Moving, Household—Fiction.
3. Email—Fiction.] I. Title.
PZ7.R71868 Ch 2002
[Fic]—dc21   2001035661

ISBN 978-0-7636-2088-2 (paperback)

2 4 6 8 10 9 7 5 3 1

Printed in the United States of America

This book was typeset in Stone Informal.

Candlewick Press
2067 Massachusetts Avenue
Cambridge, Massachusetts 02140

visit us at www.candlewick.com

q : ¬)

From: ChaseR@eureka.org
To: badadditude@hottmailer.com
Date: 10 August 5:23pm
Subject: Testing 1, 2, 3, 4, 5, 6, 7, 8, 9, 10, 11, 12, 13, 14, 15, 16, 17, 18, 19, 20

Test results: Chase can still count to 20!

Hey, Jeremy, I'm back online. At least I think. Write back to say you got this. My last three tests bounced back UNDELIVERED and USER NOT KNOWN. But I think the codes are right now that I've had a two-hour call with Isaac the Internet Wonk. [%¬7

First problem: way out here no Internet service works without a long-distance connection charge. And before that we had to install a rooftop satellite dish. But before Dad could get around to THAT, Mom made him install a water-purifier gizmo so our clothes didn't turn as pink as the drinking water. And then it turned out that our phone lines couldn't work for a modem. People had to come out and relocate lines, bury cables—whatever. Anyway, with every-thing else this move brought, getting the computer online didn't rank real high since I'm the only one who really uses it. But I'm back ON and making up for lost time! In fact, I'm even starting a newsletter . . . stay tuned.

At least I think I am. Write back and tell me you got this!
Testing 1, 2, 3, 4, 5

From: Chase Riley <ChaseR@eureka.org>
To: buddy list #1
<badadditude@hottmailer.com>, <melissa_cogdon@reachout.com>,
<onefishtwofish@ee-way.net>, <dodger2@usamericanet.com>,
<keithjopaul@penfold.postbox.edu>, <flameon@questcom.com>,
<amanda_goodhart@grapevine.com>, <topdog@midwestrescue.org>,
<redrover@setterkennel.com>, <mistermax@free-stone.com>,
<spthanks2@uinspirer.net>, <robbiem@fsgee.com>, <marko19@hottmailer.com>,
<tennessgirl@globalcom.net>, <playball@usa2day.com>,
<greentree@ethruway.net>, <lizbee@silvanst.net>, <myvalentine@kentlee.org>,
<mimhow@ureverloving.com>, <benlou@dawsonst.net>, <caynegray@glenf.org>,
<calebstheone@perrycty.com>, <allthekids@glenf.org>,
<bdreamers@livingthings.net>
Date: 10 August 5:24pm
Subject: Cicada of the Month Club E-Newsletter

VOLUME I, NO. 1

* * * * * * * * * * * * PREMIER ISSUE * * * * * * * * * * * *

```
                       \0//////>
* * * * * * * * * * * * * * /0\\\\\\> * * * * * * * * * * * * * *
```

Dear Sir or Madam: Have you ever tasted a cicada? One of nature's
most SUCKulent treats—and chock-a-block with protein! Sign up
NOW and receive this special offer from Chase's Cicada of the Month
Club. Once every 204 months (that's every seventeen years), we'll ship
to you, direct from Pickway County, half a million prime and tender
seventeen-year cicadas. That's right, those plague insects you've heard
so much about. They'll be freshly hatched, tender, juicy—you bet!—
and loud! WE GARAUNTEE IT, EVEN IF WE CAN'T SPELL GUARANTEE
WITHOUT LOOKING IT UP FOR THE MILLIONTH TIME! q:¬¡

```
                       \0//////>
* * * * * * * * * * * * * * /0\\\\\\> * * * * * * * * * * * * * *
```

Hi, everyone. Here, thanks to Mr. Hartford's computer class, e-news-letter numero unero, typed at my new record speed of 47 words per minute. (My sister timed me. She can't even do 30.) This comes to you free, SPAM included. Not available on newsstands or comic-book racks! Which title do you like better (check one):

_____ Country Living Hell [the logo could be the devil] } ; 7 / >

_____ CHASE'S LAST CHANCE [the logo could be plain-old me] q : – ∫

_____ BEYOND COLUMBUS [with a cow for a real cow town] 3 : (:))

Cast your vote and WRITE BACK! I'M FINALLY ONLINE AGAIN. It only took 4x4ever. And now, suddenly, we're having this huge lightning-cracking mother thunderstorm and I don't want the computer to get toasted, so I got to sign off NOW!

[time passing . . .]

OK, it's tomorrow. H-u-g-e storm last night. Two giant trees fell across our driveway. We didn't even know it until Dad had to walk the half mile up the gravel road to our house. So Dad unpacked his still-in-the-box, never-used-before chain saw (45 minutes trying to start it . . .), and Mallory and I carted off logs until it was way too dark.

So I know you're waiting to hear more about your friends the . . .

3

```
\0//////>  \0//////>  \0//////>  \0//////>
/0\\\\\\>  /0\\\\\\>  /0\\\\\\>  /0\\\\\\>
\0//////>  \0//////>  \0//////>  \0//////>
/0\\\\\\>  /0\\\\\\>  /0\\\\\\>  /0\\\\\\>
\0//////>  \0//////>  \0//////>  \0//////>
/0\\\\\\>  /0\\\\\\>  /0\\\\\\>  /0\\\\\\>
\0//////>  \0//////>  \0//////>  \0//////>
/0\\\\\\>  /0\\\\\\>  /0\\\\\\>  /0\\\\\\>
\0//////>  \0//////>  \0//////>  \0//////>
/0\\\\\\>  /0\\\\\\>  /0\\\\\\>  /0\\\\\\>
\0//////>  \0//////>  \0//////>  \0//////>
/0\\\\\\>  /0\\\\\\>  /0\\\\\\>  /0\\\\\\>
\0//////>  \0//////>  \0//////>  \0//////>
/0\\\\\\>  /0\\\\\\>  /0\\\\\\>  /0\\\\\\>
\0//////>  \0//////>  \0//////>  \0//////>
/0\\\\\\>  /0\\\\\\>  /0\\\\\\>  /0\\\\\\>
\0//////>  \0//  CICADAS  ////>  \0//////>
/0\\\\\\>  /0\\\\\\>  /0\\\\\\>  /0\\\\\\>
\0//////>  \0//////>  \0//////>  \0//////>
/0\\\\\\>  /0\\\\\\>  /0\\\\\\>  /0\\\\\\>
\0//////>  \0//////>  \0//////>  \0//////>
/0\\\\\\>  /0\\\\\\>  /0\\\\\\>  /0\\\\\\>
\0//////>  \0//////>  \0//////>  \0//////>
/0\\\\\\>  /0\\\\\\>  /0\\\\\\>  /0\\\\\\>
\0//////>  \0//////>  \0//////>  \0//////>
/0\\\\\\>  /0\\\\\\>  /0\\\\\\>  /0\\\\\\>
\0//////>  \0//////>  \0//////>  \0//////>
/0\\\\\\>  /0\\\\\\>  /0\\\\\\>  /0\\\\\\>
\0//////>  \0//////>  \0//////>  \0//////>
/0\\\\\\>  /0\\\\\\>  /0\\\\\\>  /0\\\\\\>
\0//////>  \0//////>  \0//////>  \0//////>
/0\\\\\\>  /0\\\\\\>  /0\\\\\\>  /0\\\\\\>
```

```
\0//////>   \0//////>   \0//////>   \0//////>
/0\\\\\\>   /0\\\\\\>   /0\\\\\\>   /0\\\\\\>
\0//////>   \0//////>   \0//////>   \0//////>
/0\\\\\\>   /0\\\\\\>   /0\\\\\\>   /0\\\\\\>
\0//////>   \0//////>   \0//////>   \0//////>
/0\\\\\\>   /0\\\\\\>   /0\\\\\\>   /0\\\\\\>
\0//////>   \0//////>   \0//////>   \0//////>
/0\\\\\\>   /0\\\\\\>   /0\\\\\\>   /0\\\\\\>
\0//////>   \0//////>   \0//////>   \0//////>
/0\\\\\\>   /0\\\\\\>   /0\\\\\\>   /0\\\\\\>
\0//////>   \0//////>   \0//////>   \0//////>
/0\\\\\\>   /0\\\\\\>   /0\\\\\\>   /0\\\\\\>
\0//////>   \0//////>   \0//////>   \0//////>
/0\\\\\\>   /0\\\\\\>   /0\\\\\\>   /0\\\\\\>
\0//////>   \0//////>   \0//////>   \0//////>
/0\\\\\\>   /0\\\\\\>   /0\\\\\\>   /0\\\\\\>
\0//////>   \0//  CICADAS  ////>   \0//////>
/0\\\\\\>   /0\\\\\\>   /0\\\\\\>   /0\\\\\\>
\0//////>   \0//////>   \0//////>   \0//////>
/0\\\\\\>   /0\\\\\\>   /0\\\\\\>   /0\\\\\\>
\0//////>   \0//////>   \0//////>   \0//////>
/0\\\\\\>   /0\\\\\\>   /0\\\\\\>   /0\\\\\\>
\0//////>   \0//////>   \0//////>   \0//////>
/0\\\\\\>   /0\\\\\\>   /0\\\\\\>   /0\\\\\\>
\0//////>   \0//////>   \0//////>   \0//////>
/0\\\\\\>   /0\\\\\\>   /0\\\\\\>   /0\\\\\\>
\0//////>   \0//////>   \0//////>   \0//////>
/0\\\\\\>   /0\\\\\\>   /0\\\\\\>   /0\\\\\\>
\0//////>   \0//////>   \0//////>   \0//////>
/0\\\\\\>   /0\\\\\\>   /0\\\\\\>   /0\\\\\\>
\0//////>   \0//////>   \0//////>   \0//////>
/0\\\\\\>   /0\\\\\\>   /0\\\\\\>   /0\\\\\\>
\0//////>   \0//////>
/0\\\\\\>   /0\\\\\\>
```

<u>click here for more.</u>

We never had these big buggers back in Columbus. And you probably won't believe me since you're not here. But are THEY ever here! The day we moved to this place, the lead story in the local paper—get this, it's called the BEAVER CREEK BEACON—was all about the seventeen-year cicadas, including cicada recipes from our local home ec expert! (More like home ICK!) She has one recipe for Cicada Pizza and another for Chirpie Cicada Chip Ice Cream. C'mon, kids, it's easy!

> Step 1: Place your container of live cicadas in the freezer for several hours. [Like you're really going to get Mom's permission.]

> Step 2: Yank off the wings and roast the bodies on a cookie sheet in a 200° oven for 1 hour, or until crispy. [Then throw out Mom's cookie sheet since you know she'll never use it again.]

The BEACON says the insects taste like asparagus only sweeter. (Like asparagus is any good to start with!) Once you roast them, you can:

➢ use them instead of chocolate chips in cookies

➢ swap the bugs in recipes that call for nuts or raisins

➢ puke just thinking about this

When we first saw our farm back at spring break, Mom kept saying how utterly quiet it seems out here. Some peeping, some wind-in-the-trees whooshing, some bubbling water. That was about it. But that was before we spent the night here and heard it all. For starters try these four critters:

1. The frogs. Talk about loud! Not just the little rubber-band-plucking *boing* of the spring peepers, but a stadium full of bullfrogs encircling the pond, belching their fight song like, I don't know, like BULLS.

2. The barred owls (ŏvŏ). They begin this howling laugh at dusk that's more like the hooting and whooping of a person who's imitating a chimpanzee. You have to hear it for yourself. "Whoo, whoo, whoo, whoo, whooooo," right up the scale.

3. Hummingbirds. Did you all know that hummingbirds are LOUD? They sound like lawn mowers down the block, but revving real fast. And they're mean! The males buzz-bomb each other, zigzagging around the bird feeders.

4. The Cicadas. To help you imagine the sound of these idiot bugs . . .

   a. Forget about the cicadas you find in the city. Or grasshoppers or crickets or any precious little buglet. Have you forgotten them? Good.

   b. Picture these, instead: Fat, two-inch-long males.

   c. Now time for math skills. Internet Fact: "In heavily infested areas, the emerging cicada population numbers a million and a half per acre." That's 1,500,000 cicadas. So, if Mr. and Mrs. Riley have a 90-acre farm, a third of the land is cornfields. Two-thirds is forest. (Cicadas especially love the forest.) If there are 1,500,000 bugs in every infested acre, how many cicadas are screaming and shouting all day long at the Riley house? BIG HINT: You may use your calculator or your earplugs.

All right, I'll tell you the answer: We're plagued with more than a billion cicadas on our land.

   But now, the sound itself.

7

d. Is it buzzing? Good guess, but no. Is it humming? If only! Chirping? Fat chance. Creaking, clicking, cheeping, trilling, chirruping? No, no, no, no, no . . . you give up? It's like

an   > (: :) Ø | (<   spaceship landing!

(that's an alien smiley). The mother ship. A fleet of mother ships. Millions of grinding and grating bug parts, sawing away like fiddles strung with barbed wire. Does that explain it? And the hotter and dryer it gets, the louder they get. Midafternoon, you can't go outside without covering your ears.

This is me wearing my Walkman, superbass and volume turned up under my ball cap, and all the cicada sound pounding down! Geddit?
& * $ # ' @ # = !   q [: - /

It's so loud, that when we call friends in the city, everyone says, "Jeez, what's that noise in the background?" Oh, nothing, IT'S JUST AN INVASION!

You think I'm making this up? I found this on the Web: Some official guy measured the cicadas' sound. Standing ten feet from a tree filled with them, his noise-o-meter read 95 decibels; when he stood under the tree, it went to 100 decibels—as loud as a subway train. Now multiply that by . . . It's noisy in these here rural parts! Who would have thought? But we didn't move here because we wanted peace and quiet. (As you remember, yours truly did not move here because yours truly wanted anything at all out here. But that's another story I do believe I told all of you over and over before we left Columbus. That's how much the fourteen-and-under opinion matters out here.)

Since we're under attack, you'll understand I have to go. But I wanted to send this right away. Talk to everybody later,

Chase

ɑː¬)

*   *   *   *   *   *   *   *   *

In our NEXT ISSUE:

> Top Ten Reasons to Move to the Country

> Top Ten Reasons to Move Back to the City

> And the answer to Today's Quiz Question:

　　　Q: Cicadas, do they sting or do they bite?

From: ChaseR@eureka.org
To: badadditude@hottmailer.com
Date: 10 August 10:38pm
Subject: You win

Dear Jeremy   –Õʃ Ô–

(I'm making smileys for everybody so I can enter them into my e-mail shortcuts. I think that will work. This one OK for you? You don't even have to read it sideways. I didn't put in the braces #, but I can if you want. For sure!)

You were the first one to write back so you win! I forgot to think of what the prize is, but you're the winner.

You're so right about Mallory. She loves it out here and that's because she DRIVES. So as much as she's here, like weekends, she says, "Oh, I wish we could have spent my first seventeen years in the country." Mallory is obviously part cicada. (I don't know what her other part is.) She's been commuting fifteen minutes to work in Lexington all summer. She leaves before the cicadas really start up and hauls her butt home right before dark when they've shut up again. She has no idea.

Mallory heads off for college in a few weeks. She'll never even think of this place as home. It'll be like a vacation lodge for her. Four years of college, she'll meet someone, she'll visit on holidays—whatever. I don't miss her yet. A sister has to be around enough before you can miss her.

I know you don't always like having three older brothers, but that means you've almost always got someone around to drive you. Funny thing out here: I've seen kids our age DRIVING their riding mowers to the store. Don't need a driver's license for that.

I gotta go. I just wanted to answer your e-mail before bed.

I'm using this one for me: q:¬)

Or me when Mom insists that I wear my cap the right way: d:−/

Or me—like now!—when someone is yelling for me to get offline so they can make a phone call: q;−|

q;−@   (me yelling, "ALL RIGHT!")

From: ChaseR@eureka.org
To: buddy list #1
Date: 11 August 9:10am
Subject: Chase's E-Newsletter/More news from your city-kid-in-the-country reporter!

VOLUME I, No. 2

*****HOT-ENOUGH-FOR-YOU? ISSUE*****

Hi, everyone! First things first, since I know you've been waiting.

TOP TEN REASONS TO MOVE TO THE COUNTRY

1. Your parents want to move there.

2. No way they're going to let you stay behind.

3. Your dad says it will be a peaceful place to write his dissertation—that is, once he finishes his classes and quits working full-time at the lab.

4. Your dogs don't have to be on leashes, and they'll love running after rabbits and swimming in the pond. (This is not on the top ten reasons the rabbits give.)

5. You always liked summer camp and think that living on a farm will be just like that, only without counselors to tell you "lights out."

6. Picking your own blackberries and raspberries for breakfast is pretty cool. (They grow wild here.)

7. You (meaning, your parents) want a slower pace of life, free of the city's hustle & bustle. (What is a bustle? Um, could it have anything to do with . . .

(o) (o)   ?)

8, 9, 10? No other reasons are currently known.

TOP TEN REASONS TO MOVE BACK TO THE CITY

1. You were right all along.

2. Your parents were wrong.

3. All your friends will still be there if you don't wait too long.

4. You won't have to start eighth grade without a single friend in the entire school, thank you very much.

5. You overestimated how much you liked summer camp. It was fun and everything, but year-round?

6. Your dogs' coats have found every tick and burr and sticker and wild-rose thorn on your property, and it takes forever to clean them.

7a. Your dogs have found every mud puddle and stinky stream and murky spot in the pond, so once you pluck out all the stuff from #6, you have to rinse them before they can go in the house.

7b. And you have to coil the hose again because it really pisses off your father if you leave it looped all over the drive.

8. There are skunks.

9. Cicadas. (THEY won't be back for seventeen years, but you better believe they've got friends and relatives: hornets, wasps, mosquitoes, and so on. If there are 5,000 mosquito larvae in a typical puddle, and Mr. and Mrs. Riley have something like 90 acres of puddles, how many . . . ?)

10. You asked your parents nicely, really, really sincerely, and promised to be a better kid, hang up your clothes, and make lots of other important sacrifices like not calling your sister a cow when she's only being an ass.

• <u>click here</u> for reasons 11–25.

• <u>click here</u> for reasons 26–50.

• <u>click here</u> for reasons 51–100,000.

Now back to the question on everyone's mind. Whassup with all Chase's friends the

Sad to report, they only last a month. They only live a few days, it's just that new ones keep emerging for weeks. So the sound is mostly gone, but you still can't go anywhere outside without stepping on their dead bodies. And the dried shells they shed are everywhere. They're clinging to our screens, the trees, leaves, your socks, your hair (if you walk under a tree). I've been sweeping the porch and the walks and the outside window ledges almost every day. Gives me the creeps! All these little deaths add up.

The only good thing (besides Cicada Pizza!) is that when a cicada lands on you, it can't sting or bite. And there's the answer to last issue's Quiz Question: THEY DON'T EVEN HAVE MOUTHS. They don't eat once they hatch as adults. They just burn up whatever root juice they've stored up while underground. And at the other end, or as my friend Lise used to say, at "the business end," of the cicada, there's no stinger. Just a squirter that leaves the eggs or the sperm. So there's everything you need for the fifth-grade science fair.

So unpacking and painting and all the rest of the moving jobs kept us inside for a lot of the cicada eruption. (We just got air conditioning.) I'll be 31 the next time they come back. Mallory will be 35, and married probably, with kids that could even be my age now. Mom and Dad will be 60 exactly. And my grandparents would have to be 80-something. Seventeen years is a long time. I won't even be living here next time they come. Who knows?

More later from Cicada $\begin{smallmatrix} \backslash 0/////> \\ /0\backslash\backslash\backslash\backslash\backslash> \end{smallmatrix}$ Central, Your Source for Everything Remote and Revolting,

Chase

q:¬)

But wait, before I sign off, I'm pasting in another e-newsletter feature: highlights of the hideous, half-witted, harebrained misdeeds here in the countryside. These come to you compliments of the BEAVER CREEK BEACON. Every week they list all the doings of the highway patrol and the sheriff's office. Real Live Law Enforcement. It's a column called "Police Activity," and it's the only part of the paper I read. It goes on for pages in among all the ads for balloon bouquets and photos of the lady basketball players. Here are two favorites, VERBATIM. (That means: Chase did not change a single word.)

CRIMES OF THE COUNTRYSIDE

>>>>>Thornview, August 3. A Baltimore Street woman told police someone threw a package of cheese against her front-door screen. No further problem followed.

>>>>>New Roscoe, August 4. A Lancaster man parked his vehicle then realized that he had left his wallet on a picnic table. As he went to retrieve his wallet, his vehicle rolled into Beaver Creek.

*   *   *   *   *   *   *   *   *

In our NEXT ISSUE:

> What's That Smell? Ask the Dogs.

> Who Knew There Were So Many Kinds of Mushrooms? They're Everywhere! (Plus easy puffball recipes from Mom's Kitchen   C=:¬p   )

> And the answer to Today's Quiz Question:

>   Q: Will Chase quit pretending that he hates living in the country because we all know that he really likes it, except there's just stuff in the city (like us) that he really likes, too?

From: ChaseR@eureka.org
To: −õʃô−
Date: 11 August 4:55pm
Subject: To be continued . . .

Hey, Jeronimo,

I wanted to add a few more things just to you. Promise, no more about the cicadas. (I WISH!)

One thing that BUGS me about e-mail is I end up forgetting to answer questions people write me, and I end up asking stuff that never gets answered. I guess I just hate not hanging out together.

But I did remember that I need you to send me another copy of our last tape. I can't find the box it's packed in. Or maybe it got chucked into the garage sale. I still want to practice some of our songs, even though I know I won't be jamming with you and Doughnut and Chris anytime soon. (How is Doughnut? Haven't heard from him. Haven't heard from lots of kids. Doughnut isn't away at camp or anything, is he?) I haven't found anyone who gives guitar lessons and can drive over, and remember what happened that time I tried to bike to your place holding my guitar?

Been working with Dad on yard stuff. Not so much planting because we have this deal with another farmer who takes care of the corn. He keeps half the profit. At first I was all excited because you know how much I love corn, but it ends up that we grow the variety that's for horses. Not that we have horses. Never mind. Still, lots of other farms have stands, and we've had great corn on the cob. Almost every night. There's even a corn festival nearby right before school starts. You should come out for that.

So I've been weeding, weed whacking, hacking down poison ivy vines (I'm the only one who's not allergic—SO FAR), lugging rotted wood and junk to burn. We've really made a lot of progress.

What else? I went mountain biking twice with this kid Aaron who lives as close as anyone. Around here there are dozens of places to just ride and ride, if you don't mind getting whipped in the head by low tree limbs and wearing cobweb hair nets as you speed along. But you don't really get to talk much with anyone while you're biking.

Also met another kid who has beagles named Jeff. HIS name is Jeff, and there are four beagles but I didn't catch all their names except one, Copper. Actually, our dogs met in the woods and we ended up meeting just getting the dogs to unmeet.

I'm back. I had to go with Mom to the doctor's for a tetanus shot since I BARELY cut myself on some old fence wire this morning, but I guess I was due for one. The nurse even gave me a lollipop.

That's so cool about your brother taking the radio job. What kind of music do they play, or is it just a station where they talk all the time? We've got this one construction guy here, Sid, who's spackling and fixing these big cracks in our ceiling, and he always has the radio tuned to these ignoramuses calling in their opinions, spilling their guts for all of Ohio to hear. Mom makes him change the channel whenever she walks in.

I'm going swimming at this giant quarry this morning, me and these two kids my mom introduced me to at the post office. (Get this: She just walked over to them and said, "Hi, we're new in town, let's all meet." My mom, totally UNCOOL. But it turned out this family had just moved out here, too.) It's a pretty awesome place to swim—some company used to dig up sand from it. But now it's just filled with water. This one kid's dad owns a big portion of it, and his family's going. The sheriff is supposed to keep everyone else out because high school kids always trespass, smash their beer bottles on the rocks, and even dive off the cliffs. They're insane. The water's full of huge boulders.

I'm being picked up in a few minutes. More tomorrow!

. . . _ (:) -○   (me with scuba mask)

From: ChaseR@eureka.org
To: badattitude@hottmailer.com
Date: 12 August 12:21pm
Subject: Camp Chase

–õ∫Ô–

I cued my last message but forgot to send it. So here it is with this one, too. Those guys arrived early. When you're here sometime, I'll ask Sean and Sam if they'll take us to the quarry. The best part is how clear the water is. You can tread water and see your feet. Not like the pond here, where this cloud of gray muck floats up wherever you step.

q: ¬)

P.S. You ARE going to get out here sometime. Soon.

From: ChaseR@eureka.org
To: keithjopaul@penfold.postbox.edu
Date: 12 August 12:21pm
Subject: Camp Chase

Dear Paul,

Are you and Keith back from tennis camp? I was in town over the weekend and tried to hook up with you guys, but no one answered the phone. Mom decided to drag us all in for a party at my cousin Jill's, who's got a swimming scholarship for some college like UCLA or USC, or maybe it's USDA she's mooooving to. 3 : (:))

I'm not her favorite cousin, I don't think, because I remember her when she used to lose lots of races, and we used to be on the same swim team at Hampton Swim Club. Didn't Jo also swim backstroke with her when they were in middle school?

So if you are back, write me. Or come on out for a day at Camp Chase. We got lots of stuff to do, except our version of tennis is throwing tennis balls to our dogs, who like to fetch them from the pond. They also try to fetch frogs, which I think they think are just tennis balls that have hatched.

Bye!

Chase

q : ¬)

From: ChaseR@eureka.org
To: flameon@questcom.com, tennessgirl@globalcom.net, playball@usa2day.com, dodger2@usamericanet.com
Date: 12 August 12:21pm
Subject: :=8 | You baboons out there?

You guys are in serious danger of having your subscription to my e-newsletter canceled and missing out on all the news from Beaver Creek.

Write back! Snail mail, even. I've heard from everyone else but you four! Come on. I miss seeing you so, I've got to hear from you.

Chase

q:¬)

From: ChaseR@eureka.org
To: amanda_goodhart@grapevine.com
Date: 13 August 8:16pm
Subject: No can do

Dear Amanda,

No, our computer, or maybe it's our Internet people, whatever, won't let us do instant messaging from here. Plus my folks won't let me stay on the computer long enough to even type my name. The latest rule is I have to keyboard whatever I want to say, make sure no one's on the phone, then log on, send, and log off before my mom

@@@@ : -]

or my dad

(: 7 (|)

needs the phone. And if, on the off chance Mallory

& : -)= 8

is home, I might as well try to find a pay phone to log on. Wait, we don't have phone booths out here!

So I can't join in, not for now anyway. Thanks for writing back! Maybe I'll see you at Lindsey's party next weekend.

Bye for now,

Chase

q : - (

From: ChaseR@eureka.org
To: badadditude@hottmailer.com
Date: 13 August 8:16pm
Subject: Deer!

–õʃÔ–

You better not be kidding me about performing at the swim club. Sweet! How long do you get? And they're paying you 50 real dollars not just 50 snack-bar coupons? Maybe Mom will drive me in for the weekend. I don't expect to get up and just play with you three (like Doughnut would even let me), but I could come to the party. Totally cool, even if it's only a one-time gig.

I walk Pirate and Bonner every day, and these last few weeks, we always spot deer just staring at us across the meadow or the cornfield. I'm shocked at how good the dogs are. I give the old STAY command as soon as I spot a deer, and for some reason, they know it's important and they stay. But they're also pretty interested in the little dotted piles of deer crap and the deer trails that cut through the forest. But these deer are majestic. (There's no word for it. The thesaurus tool came up with "exalted" or "stirring" among some useless others.) But they're something besides just "awesome." For one thing, they're huge. I've never seen such a large wild animal except in a zoo. And they look very proud, sort of like Mrs. Winston from history class, craning her head to the max so she could see in all directions. And I don't know how they do this, but it seems the whole field, and even the air around them, all freezes when they stop and turn their heads to see who's there.

Most of the time we spot family groups, like one bigger deer with two smaller ones. But they always turn and tear off after 30 seconds or so. We try not to move at all, but our smell wafts over to them. We can never get close enough to convince them that we wouldn't harm them.

Last weekend Mom cut up a bunch of her old tights, and we tucked hair clippings that Dad brought home from the barbershop inside them, plus pieces of Irish Spring soap that the deer hate (it IS kind of stinky), and we hung them like ornaments on the rhododendrons—Mom's favorite plant, and also the deer's favorite. I suggested singing, "O Tanenbaum, o Tanenbaum, how lovely are thy branches," but, no, this was serious farm work. Ho, ho, ho.
$* < | : \neg) > > >$

So all that's supposed to repel the deer. They also won't go near the smell of urine. Some guy from the county extension service came out and gave us all this free advice about our orchard (we have some old apple trees and a few pear trees), including ways to "discourage" deer. (So I say, "Yeah, like telling them they're stupid and they'll never get into college or amount to anything." That didn't make anyone laugh, and THAT discouraged ME.) q : - (

Anyway, Bonner and Pirate were walking with us, and the guy says, "Have your dogs come out to the orchard here to do their business. Dog urine keeps deer away as well as most things. The human stuff works, too, if you ever have some folks over for a party and happen to be chugging some serious beer."

Dad didn't like that remark. (💣 ∠ 💣): "Not smart, suggesting having a beer party in front of a MINOR."

A keg night sounded OK to me, but Dad just gave me the look, too. I can just see the BEACON running a headline by that advice columnist: "Fool-proof Pee-pee Preventatives in the War against Deer."

When Mom came back from the local beauty shop, she found out there was a waiting list for the hair cuttings. Everyone's got deer munching their crops.

Say hi to everyone there. We'll probably drive in for a few Buckeye games this fall. (It's only an hour and ten minutes away—like 60 miles—though it feels like 600.) Dad says his old boss has tickets he never uses. I'll let you know.

Bye for now,

Chase

q : ¬)

From: ChaseR@eureka.org
To: badadditude@hottmailer.com
Date: 16 August 7:01pm
Subject: Sick! cayduhs!

–õ¡Ô–

How about this for a life? Learned this on some strange-rangers home page that's all about insects.

THE LIFE CYCLE OF A

1. Suck roots for seventeen years.

2. Climb out and shed your little outside skeleton.

3. Dry off and start shrieking (boys only).

4. Find some other cicada who's depositing the other half of the stuff that makes babies (which, by the way, slices up the branches of the young trees so they'll drop and deliver the larvae things down to the earth again).

5. Drop dead. Period. The end. Over and out.

GET A LIFE!

Oh, I forgot to mention flying—that's a part of their short lives, too, but they're total amateurs. They're too big and too heavy and their huge red eyes need Visine. And they have exactly ZERO practice at flying before it's time to crash-land and die.

So, Jeremy, your idea of making a horror flick about them is perfect. We just have to time everything perfectly so we can be ready to shoot the year we turn 31 and they reappear. I'll do the camera work and you can be the animal handler. We can have this scene where they devour a barnyard full of pigs or carry off little kids like those flying monkeys in THE WIZARD OF OZ. We have plenty of time to write the screenplay.

```
\0//////>  \0//////>  \0//////>  \0//////>
/0\\\\\\\>  /0\\\\\\\>  /0\\\\\\\>  /0\\\\\\\>
\0//////>  \0//////>  \0//////>  \0//////>
/0\\\\\\\>  /0\\\\\\\>  /0\\\\\\\>  /0\\\\\\\>
 :(:)(      :(:)(       :(:)(       :(:)(
\0//////>  \0//////>  \0//////>  \0//////>
/0\\\\\\\>  /0\\\\\\\>  /0\\\\\\\>  /0\\\\\\\>
\0//////>  \0//////>  \0//////>  \0//////>
/0\\\\\\\>  /0\\\\\\\>  /0\\\\\\\>  /0\\\\\\\>
```

(four pigs being carried away in a swarm of cicadas)

Chase

q:-@ helllpppp!

From: ChaseR@eureka.org
To: buddy list #1
Date: 23 August 1:28pm
Subject: Chase's E-Newsletter/More news from your country reporter!

VOLUME I, NO. 3

✶✶✶✶✶✶SPECIAL PRE-SCHOOL EDITION✶✶✶✶✶✶

(No, that doesn't mean if you're going into the eighth grade you're sent back to preschool in the country.)

Hey, everybody, welcome to my latest issue, which I also thought of calling my "fresh air" edition, since there's a new rule at the house: for every hour I'm on the computer, I have to go outside for an hour. I'm saving up for a laptop so I can do both at the same time. So, first of all:

ANSWER TO LAST ISSUE'S QUESTION (Anyone remember what the question was? It was about hating or loving country life.): Here's the answer: Chase is having a loving-it-and-hating-it relationship with it, and it's called culture shock, OK? Which means, moving to the country is moving to another planet, even though it's only 60 miles away. So I'm in shock. Here are some shock waves taken right from my brain:

$\bigvee\bigvee\bigvee\bigvee\bigvee\bigvee\bigvee\bigvee\bigvee\bigvee\bigvee\bigvee\bigvee\bigvee\bigvee\bigvee\bigvee\bigvee\bigvee$
$\bigvee\bigvee\bigvee\bigvee\bigvee\bigvee\bigvee\bigvee\bigvee\bigvee\bigvee\bigvee\bigvee\bigvee\bigvee\bigvee\bigvee\bigvee\bigvee$

And now, SOME SHOCKING DIFFERENCES:
/\/\/\ Shocking, as in real shocks: When we lose electricity in a storm, we don't have any water, either, because our well uses a pump. Nice.

No toilet flushing. Extra nice. So we have to fill buckets of water whenever it starts thundering. Which has been frequently. "Chase, can you reset the VCR and reprogram all the clocks," yada yada yada. /\/\/\

\/\/\/ Not so funny: Some neighbors don't have running water or electricity ever. They use propane for power, and they have these giant cisterns of water. \/\

/\/\/\ Sort of funny: Whenever you pass someone on the road, there's a Pickway County signal: the driver lifts one finger off the steering wheel in greeting. I always watch and they always do. Even my MnD have picked up the habit, too. When I finally apply for my driver's license, that'll be on the test. /\/\/\/\/\/\/\/\/\/\/\/\/\/\

\/\/\/ Unbelievable: Some Amish kids drive here in their horse-drawn cart and park near our general store and stand there all day in the heat in their long-sleeve wool clothes selling corn. \/\/\/\/\/\/\/\/\

/\/\/\ Definitely funny: Lots of houses here have deer statues in their front yard or out by their pond. Not like anybody really wants real deer in their yard! Huh? Besides, everyone out here hunts deer. Confused?!

\/\/\/ Funnier yet: When my aunt and uncle visited, we all went to the pottery festival (lots of ceramic factories used to be in this region on account of the sand quarries). It was another chance to eat homemade pies and bratwursts and see a queen get crowned. A little girl in maybe fourth grade got to be Miss Betty Crockery or something. Queen Crock-Pot. Princess Pinch-pot. I can't remember. She didn't get a fancy ear-of-corn scepter like Miss Silver Queen gets at the corn festival. Tough BREAK for the pottery queen. /\/\/\/\/\/\/\/\/\

/\/\/\ Shocked me as all get-out: At the IGA nearest to us and at the gas station, they have three or four soda machines sitting outside. So you've got Coke and Hawaiian Punch and Mountain Dew, etc., and then in one machine, it's nightcrawlers, crickets, grub worms—LIVE BAIT. Put in your dollar and out drops your carton of bait. And now . . .

@@@@@SCHOOL DAZE@@@@@

The big thing on everyone's mind, especially my parents': What subjects should Chase take at his new school? Pickway Middle School offers a few different things. A sampling from the catalog I imagine they will send me.

☐ Basic Tractor Repair (I'll need this if Dad keeps breaking ours.)

☐ Poultry Science (Finally, the answer to questions such as "Which came first, the chicken or the egg?")

☐ Beyond 4-H (4-I, 4-J, 4-K, etc.—a big major out here)

☐ Animal Husbandry—or for the boys, Animal Wifery

☐ Hayfever, Pollen, Mildew, Ragweed: Is It Your Imagination?

☐ Foreign Language/Choices include:

   a. How to read instruction manuals written in "English" by someone in another country who can't speak it.

   b. Duck calling (also wild turkey)

   c. Dog training (Class limited to four, since it's mostly beagles out here and they're not exactly honors students. They're always escaping and it takes most everyone in the study hall to go round them up.)

☐ Human Ecology (required) (This is supposed to be sex ed, like we have in Columbus, but here I think we start with the lively story of how babies come from the cabbage patch.)

☐ Web Design (No, not computers, spiders. It's an honors biology course. Hardly anyone has a computer here. Sweeney's General Store doesn't even have a computer cash register. It's an adding machine. But get this: If you forget to bring enough money, you can pay them back later. Just like stores in Columbus, right?)

☐ Shop (Since everyone here already knows all the mechanical tool stuff you're supposed to learn in shop class, this course is a weekly field trip to Hopewell Run Mall, where there's a confusing number of big stores to experience. Prerequisite: your dad's credit card.)

So, these could be a few of my electives. I have to take English, history, phys ed, math, maybe music. I have a new students' meeting soon just to "get acquainted." I bet we'll make name tags with little stickers to show our hobbies. (SAVE ME.)

There's more to say, but I'll send this out now so I can hear back from YOU. Take care, everyone,

Chase

q:¬)

$\star$ $\star$ $\star$ $\star$ $\star$ $\star$ $\star$ $\star$ $\star$

In our NEXT ISSUE:

> "50 Years Ago This Week," highlights from the BEAVER CROAK BEACON, including a visit with "Miss Oklahoma," the hippopotamus that visited our country fair.   (^ , _____ , ^)

(©   ©   )

(^^^^^^^^)

> Chicken-of-the-woods, this orange mushroom growing on our willow tree that the guy who farms our property is trying to convince us to eat. It's the color of those circus peanut candies your mom serves when her friends come over to play cards. But these are huge, like bookshelves. Stand by for the results of our taste test. (Right.)

> And the answer to Today's Quiz Question:

a. How long will it take Chase's mom and dad to make enough money so they can keep this house as just a place to come for weekends and buy another house back in Columbus?

b. How long will Chase keep asking stupid questions?

From: ChaseR@eureka.org
To: badattitude@hottmailer.com
Date: 23 August 3:21pm
Subject: re: Summer School!!!!!!!

–õ¡Ô–

I know what you mean. Even before summer's over, your mom is taking you shopping for school clothes. We don't even have three months of vacation anymore. Like that's fair. There are 180 days of school, which is about half of the 365 total. Jeremy, wouldn't you rather go to school seven days a week from November through April if you could have a six-month vacation that lasted from May all the way through October? I would! Doesn't your dad know someone on the school board who could make that happen?

I guess overall, summer has been decent. Could have been more decent for all kinds of reasons, like, for one, if you were around. I remember how it is to work for a relative. But your uncle's paying you at least. And cash, amigo man, is cash. Save up. You should have taken up guitar instead of keyboards. All I have to buy these days is new strings.

Got to run. I'll write later,

q≥:¬\ (bedhead)

From: ChaseR@eureka.org
To: badadditude@hottmailer.com
Date: 23 August 9:01pm
Subject: Happy Birthday Cookies

Dear –Õ¡Ô–

Happy Birthday tomorrow. I sent you off a package that you might even get if my Dad remembered to mail it. I'll check his car. Nothing much, but happy birthday.

In case your mom forgot to make a cake, here's the recipe you've been after from the lady in the BEAVER CREEK BACON. (That's what becomes of the pigs after the cicadas carry them off in our movie.) There's also one for Crispy Critter Treats, which are just Rice Krispies Treats with bugs dumped in the goo.

First, preheat oven to 375°. [I love this new e-mail program. I can find all the symbols like the degrees circle and everything.]

CHOCOLATE CHIRPIE CHIP COOKIES

2 1/4 cups flour
1 tsp. baking soda
1 tsp. salt
1 cup butter, softened
3/4 cup sugar
3/4 cup brown sugar
1 tsp. vanilla
2 eggs
1 12-ounce bag chocolate chips
1 cup chopped nuts
1/2 cup dry-roasted crickets or cicadas
[or why not just use spiders, moths,
water beetles, bees, ants—your choice! ꝗ : ¬@]

In small bowl, combine flour, baking soda,and salt; set aside.

In large bowl, combine butter, sugar, brown sugar,
and vanilla; beat until creamy [or you're dizzy].

Beat in eggs. Gradually add flour mixture and insects,
mix well. Stir in chocolate chips and chopped nuts.

Scoop teaspoon-sized drops onto ungreased cookie
sheet. Bake for 8–10 minutes. Set aside to cool.
[Like in the trash can so the < : 3) ~ ~ ~ ~ can enjoy them.]

From: ChaseR@eureka.org
To: topdog@midwestrescue.org
Date: 23 August 9:02pm
Subject: Hey! ∑ : - <   (that's supposed to be a smiley dog)

Dear Carolyne:

/ ü \
  ∧

That's a better dog, but still not very happy looking. I'll work on it.

How are you? How's everything at the shelter? One thing I really
miss (ONE THING? There are lots of things!) about living so far
from Columbus is working with you. I don't think there's anything
like a shelter nearby, but there is an animal control person and a
dog pound in the county seat. (I'm going to sit in the county seat
one day just to say I put my butt there.) He runs a picture of some
adoptable dog in the BEAVER CREEK BEACON each week, but I
don't know how much good that does. From what I can tell, free
puppies and free kittens signs are everywhere. You wouldn't like it,
Carolyne. Plenty of beagles and hunting dogs are kept outside in
pens. I see dogs tied out by their doghouses—all day and night.
There aren't a lot of fences to keep dogs safe. The fields are full of
cats, just having litter after litter. Not a lot of dog training. Not a lot
of letting them be in the family pack, as you always explain.

Pirate and Bonner love it here. They're glad to be off leashes. We
have 90 acres, so they just hike with me all over the place. I hardly
need to use any of the training routines you taught us. We've got a

38

couple creeks for the dogs to swim in, and that makes them act like they're all retriever instead of just part. And we have lots of animal scents to sniff out (skunk, groundhog, chipmunk, squirrel, raccoon, and whatever else digs holes and climbs trees), and that makes them act like they're all hound. You remember Pirate was the shy one in the litter, but he loves it here as much as Bonner does, who's turned out to be a real people-person. I don't know what he's going to do when school starts, because at home he's always next to me. I cut the meadows on our riding mower, and he lies in the center of the field supervising. He listens to me practice guitar. Bonner is one busy dog.

So I just wanted to write and tell you we're all fine, and that I wish I could still volunteer there. One day I'll get someone to drive us in to visit. And if one of my favorite dogs is still there—like Domino—I'm convincing my folks we have room now for a third dog. OR MORE!

Your friend,

Chase

q:¬)   and   [/'p̱'\]   and   [/'ḇ'\]

(Those are better dog smileys, though it looks like Bonner and Pirate are wearing earmuffs.)

From: ChaseR@eureka.org
To: melissa_cogdon@reachout.com (/ °¬° \ )
Date: 23 August 3:21pm
Subject: Save me!

Dear Melissa:

Thanks for your e-mail. Everyone's so busy it seems like if I'm not there, I'm just plain old not there. (Which is how I feel, but you know what I mean. I mean, I'M busy, too!) I know we're not next-door neighbors anymore and I know I didn't dance with you even once at the pool party, but I figured we should still keep in touch a little.

Pretty soon there will be e-mail where you can see the person on your screen. Maybe there already is for people with megabucks. But I'm going to write any chance I can get online. (Mallory just left to visit some friends and then onto Kent State yesterday, so that frees up the phone line about 59 minutes out of every hour.)

Shoot, I forgot to get sweet corn from our neighbors before Mom gets home. Got to dash. I'll write you again in a half hour.

From: ChaseR@eureka.org
To: melissa_cogdon@reachout.com (/ °¬° \ )
Date: 23 August 5:50pm
Subject: I'm back. Guess you're not home.

OK. Mom pulled in right as I got home. Made it. So I'm free again.

Melissa, you really got your lifeguard certification? I thought you had to be sixteen? My mom used to do that in college. She even had to perform CPR twice and saved two kids' lives.   __/ \○__

Here's something sicko. It just happened this morning so I have to tell you. I met this kid at our general store talking to the guy who runs it, Mr. Sweeney. (He and his wife—they're really nice—run the place. The first time I went in, I thought they had a pet shop because I heard all these bird calls coming from the back. Turns out Mr. Sweeney whistles while he works. For real. He can trill and warble and twitter, imitating all kinds of birds. I don't know what kinds, but I'm sure he does.)

Anyway, the sicko part: So this kid is telling Mr. Sweeney about this coyote he saw on their driveway last night. You never see coyotes around here. Some people say we don't even have coyotes, just wild dogs that get people all excited. (Kind of like your dog! Just kidding! I'm sure Maxie /@ ♠ @\ has calmed down by now.) But this kid swears it was a coyote, the first one he's ever seen. So after saying how beautiful it was, all shiny and gold, and how clear and brilliant its eyes were, and how smart and proud it looked, and on and on since the coyote wasn't even 20 feet away, he says—I swear this is true—he says: "Lord, that animal was so beautiful, I only wish I'd had my gun with me."

Here he's all amazed and inspired talking about this creature, and how the coyote was just gazing calmly back at him, and then . . . he's sorry he didn't blast the thing between the eyes? New law in the country: If it's beautiful, shoot it. HUH?

This is a kid about our age. Now maybe I could see how someone might consider shooting if a coyote was tearing up the chicken house or attacking. And so, Melissa, Culture Shock strikes again, right between MY eyes!

As you might guess, I didn't ask the kid's name or suggest that he become my new best friend. Actually I could use a best friend out here. You'd qualify if your folks got the same dim idea MnD did when they moved us to the country. Right.

Lots of things are different here. There aren't even a thousand people in our mini-village. Junction? Townito? Hamlet? (There are lots of pigs.) I don't think our whole county has even a quarter of the population back in Columbus. But, hey, we DO have tractor-pulling contests the first Saturday of every month all summer long—try to beat that! I need to add that to my list of Top Ten Reasons to Move to the Country.

One really good reason: having your own pond to swim in even AFTER Labor Day when all the city pools close. Our pond's pretty clear now, too. When I'm swimming around with the dogs, I can see their feet paddling underwater. And even though you didn't

42

ask, the answer is yes, Melissa, skinny-dipping is not just permit-
ted, it's REQUIRED.

So come on out to swim or pick apples or anything! It would be fun
to see you. Convince Gary to drive you someday. It's not like your
brother can't take a break from his skateboarding for an hour
drive. Tell him he can skateboard down our driveway, which has a
huge hill. Just don't mention it's gravel.

Bye for now! Thanks for writing back. Miss seeing you around,

Chase

q:¬)

From: ChaseR@eureka.org
To: melissa_cogdon@reachout.com (/ °¬° \ )
Date: 23 August 9:33pm
Subject: Re: Pulling my leg

No, it's not a tractor tug o' war, which is what I thought, too. It's just hundreds of tractors from all over, lots of them really ancient and gigantic. One at a time, they get hitched up to this flatbed, which has a monster weight on it that moves forward toward the tractor as the tractor speeds ahead, making it heavier and heavier to pull until the tractor spins its wheels or tips up trying to go forward. Mostly it's 900 decibels per eardrum, clouds of black smoke, and a chance for the Lions Club to grill bratwursts.

And it goes from about nine in the morning until midnight, since after each tractor competes, the dirt Zamboni machine has to regrade the surface so that the track's smooth. Last time we had one, I fell asleep to the sound of the revving engines and dreamed of the day that I, too, could enter our little Sears Craftsman riding mower . . .

From: ChaseR@eureka.org
To: riley79@kentstate.edu &:^) |
Date: 11 September 4:02pm
Subject: Testing, testing . . .

Mallory,

Is your mailbox up and running there? E-mail back and say you got this. Are there actually 78 other Rileys at Kent State? Seems weird. How big is that school?

Your bro,

q:¬)

P.S. Pick your very own MRS (Mallory Riley smiley).

#(8¬o)

or

&8^/)

or

#(:¬{})   (bad hair day, lots of lipstick)

or how about this sideways Princess Leia look?   @(°¬°)@

45

From: ChaseR@eureka.org
To: riley79@kentstate.edu
Date: 13 September 9:03pm
Subject: FW: Testing, testing . . .

\# (: ¬ { })

Did you fail the test? WRITE BACK. Testing, testing . . . are you
there?

q : ¬ |

From: ChaseR@eureka.org
To: buddy list #1
Date: 13 September 9:03pm
Subject: Chase's E-Newsletter / Special Bulletin . . .

_____ , , , ˄ . . ˄ , , , _____

* * * * * * * * * *SPECIAL BULLETIN* * * * * * * * * *

Three people said I made up the last CRIMES OF THE COUNTRY-SIDE report, and I swear I do not make these up. I copy them word for word, from the BEAVER UP-SHIT-CREEK-WITHOUT-A-PADDLE BEACON. Here are two more I was holding for the next e-newsletter, but I'll send now.

CRIMES OF THE COUNTRYSIDE

>>>>>Cliffside, August 6. A Fairland Road man reported that someone had stolen one bulb out of his strand of Christmas lights. [Was he just taking them down or just putting them up . . . or what? Readers want to know! It's not even Christmas-in-July! I am allowed to add the part in brackets. q : ¬)]

>>>>>Beaver Creek, August 7. Police responded to a disturbance at the Duke service station, where a subject was angry about the price of beer. He was advised by police to leave the premises.

More Later!

Chase

q : ¬)

From: ChaseR@eureka.org
To: –õ¡ô–
Date: 17 September 6:09pm
Subject: School

Dear Jeronimony,

Your reading list sounds a lot like mine. So does your schedule. The state probably makes all eighth graders suffer through a lot of the same courses whether they live in the city or out in the sticks. I had to switch to Spanish since we don't have Latin here. I've had enough Latin, anyway, since what else is there if you can translate the sayings on money and sing "Twinkle, Twinkle, Little Star":
☆ Mica, mica, parvae stella, ☆ mirror quanum istanbella . . . ☆

I don't think Latin helps at all with English, but you know my parents, always finding something to help their son with his Academic Challenges. Gym should be interesting at Beaver Creek. My guess is six weeks of square dancing and then six weeks of round dancing and then six of triangle dancing. And maybe fishing—that's a sport, isn't it? And then making pickles, just so the girls won't feel left out? Actually, I like all the teachers so far, and the school building used to be the high school (the high school got a new building), and so it's gigantizoid. We have huge lockers, a library that has probably never discarded a book ever, a gym as big as an airplane hangar (and almost as empty), and this huge Hall of Fame showcase right when you walk in with old photos and trophies of athletes. Beaver Creek was three times All-State Football Champs. Seriously. But all the memorabilia junk ends around 1960. At first I thought, well, maybe they've just had sucky teams for the last 40 years, but then I figured that the new high school probably only had room for the most recent stars.

I said I'd have the grill ready when Mom walked in. Shoot! Time for major pyromania!

q: ¬)

From: ChaseR@eureka.org
To: riley79@kentstate.edu
Date: 18 September 4:44pm
Subject: I hate to send you this, but . . .

Hey Mall,

Thanks for answering my last one. I know you don't want me writing long e-mails because you feel guilty since you don't have time to answer. Sorry. This one can't be short. It's not good news. They told me you are not to hear a word about this now because they think you have enough stress moving away and starting school. I don't agree—I mean, you probably have lots of stressful stuff, but I know you'd want to know. Do NOT tell them I told you!

I'm going to spit it out. He's going to be all right, but Bonner was shot yesterday. We don't know who did it and we didn't see it happen. We didn't even hear gunfire, I don't think. Bonner was out of our sight for, maybe, ten minutes while we were raking weeds out of the pond—Bonner and Pirate were swimming around and sniffing the bank for muskrats—and suddenly they were gone. So a few minutes later Dad called them and they didn't come, and we started racing around, all of us calling their names in different directions. But we didn't even know where to look. Ten minutes passed, but it seemed like forever because we were all running and shouting and worrying what could have happened to the dogs.

So we ran to the house, and suddenly there was Bonner sitting on the porch, looking the way he does when he's been yelled at. We were so relieved that no one yelled, of course, but then Mom suddenly was, like, gasping, "Oh my god!" because she saw these two holes in his fur—round holes, not even flaps of skin, just blueberry-size holes, and not bleeding. Mom was really crying. And I was, too, not only because of this wound, but I started thinking where's Pirate? We weren't even sure at that point that a bullet had done this, but I kept thinking that if Bonner had been wounded, maybe Pirate wasn't back because he'd been killed.

Dad and I were halfway down the drive to take Bonner to the vet, when we saw Pirate bouncing up the drive, wagging his tail and smiling as if to say, "Hey, what's the big deal!" We inspected him real quickly—he was fine—so we put him in the car, too, and all drove to the vet.

It was not a bite or a tear (it really looked like that); it's two holes from a bullet—a .22, which the vet says is pretty standard for hunting—and the bullet went in and out of his skin. Someone must have fired at him from above, like from a porch or a tree, and the bullet glanced off his back, ripping through loose skin (you know, like if you pulled the dog's fur away from his body and made that flap of skin). A different angle and Bonner would have been killed or crippled.

Bonnerboy's stitched up now. We're giving him antibiotics. The vet says he'll heal fine. They mend up a lot of shot dogs.

At first, I couldn't believe it. I still can't. I hate this place. Who wants to live somewhere where people shoot dogs?

So at dinner I said we had to fence in the whole property, or a huge enclosed part of it, or something to keep the dogs in and people out. We can't afford that, I understand that, whatever. I guess it isn't feasible—that's MnD's word. But it isn't FEASIBLE to have your dog shot, is it? So what if something isn't feasible? Don't you still have to find a way to do it anyway? Or try?

The vet says country people have this unwritten law that they can shoot dogs that trespass on their property, especially if there's live-stock involved. I don't know where the dogs went, but you know they wouldn't have been chasing sheep or chickens. I KNOW IT. And they weren't gone that long!

But like I said, Bonner's going to be fine.

I hope this news doesn't really make you stress out or get angry. E-mail me back just to set up a time to call, and I'll grab the phone before MnD do. I'll keep you posted on how Bonner's doing. Really, I think he's fine. Hope you are, too.

Your bro,

Chase

ɹ:¬.

From: ChaseR@eureka.org
To: riley79@kentstate.edu
Date: 19 September 8:03pm
Subject: Thanks a lot!

So now I get in trouble for doing the nice thing by telling you and you end up calling Mom and Dad. Great!

It's not like they told you anything I hadn't already e-mailed you.

They were the ones who weren't going to tell you in the first place.

Thanks for believing me. That's the last time I'm trusting you.

Come home more often if you want to know what's going on.

q;¬/ -1   (That's me giving you the finger, in case you were wondering.)

From: ChaseR@eureka.org
To: riley79@kentstate.edu
Date: 19 September 9:18pm
Subject: Update

I'm not really THAT mad anymore, Mallory, because I know it's just that you were more concerned about Bonner than about me, and maybe that's OK. But couldn't you have faked it and called for some other reason and just pretended to ask about the dogs and see if MnD would have said something? The answer is yes, you could have. Whatever. Sometimes you act like you're queen. You don't rule. You could apologize.

Bonner's leaving his stitches alone. We have this lampshade-gizmo to attach on his collar when we're gone (so he won't lick or bite at the wounds). While I'm at school, I keep thinking about him in it—he looks like he's got on the satellite dish we mounted on the roof. Half the places he likes to sleep—like under our chairs or beneath my desk—he can't squeeze into and he bonks the collar and looks up at you as if he's saying, "Why did you rearrange the furniture again?"

At breakfast this morning I said, "If I ever find out who shot him, I'll . . ." and I guess I paused too long, because then Dad said: "What? What would you do, son? I'm curious." So I say, "Why are you singling me out? Like you wouldn't do anything if you found the person?" Then Dad gives me his professor tone: "Well, I'm not sure it's always so easy to achieve any kind of justice." So I say, "For you!" which was his cue to make me leave the table.

Justice? Like that's something MnD are suddenly concerned about? If they were, I so happen to have a list of creepy shit they've pulled on me that they can start JUSTICE-ifying. So on the way to school (I was late), we continued discussing what we'd do if we learned who shot Bonner. "Could the person have had a reason?" Dad asked. "Like what if Bonner was killing chickens?" I know he doesn't think that's likely because we don't even know anyone around us who HAS a chicken house. But Bonner WAS briefly out of our sight. Of course, nobody suggested shooting the person or even wounding them to even up things. Maybe we should get money, but not just for vet bills—REAL money to make the shooter feel how wrong he was. Like $50,000 or something.

I said the person should have his guns confiscated and his hunting license taken away forever. The person shouldn't be allowed to have any weapons at all. Dad said he was pretty sure there weren't laws like that, and how would you enforce them anyway since guns are so easy to get and to hide and people hire lawyers and the cases take forever to get to court and then there are huge costs, and here's the worst: Dad said the court would only award you the "replacement cost" of the dog. Like the $45 we donated to the shelter for Bonner—45 bucks! That can't be the way the law really works. Dad thinks he's a professor of everything, but I know he's wrong about this.

So we have to learn to live with the idea that this INCIDENT (how about that bogus-sounding word) happened and there's no making it better.

Another long e-mail. So don't write back. But I'm just going to write as much as I want because you're the only other person who understands MnD, and it wouldn't hurt you to listen some since I'm here and you're not.

Study hard. Don't worry about Bonner. I'll do that. You're still my sister so I love you.

Bye,

Chase

????q: ¬? (me, asking too many questions)

From: ChaseR@eureka.org
To: riley79@kentstate.edu
Date: 19 September 10:45pm
Subject: Forgot one thing

One more thing. I know, I should be doing homework, but I can't concentrate right now. Anyway, I thought you'd think this was interesting, something you could use on sharing day in your women's studies class.

Bonner's vet is a she and she owns the clinic nearest to us. First thing she says when we arrived, "I'm Dr. Tanners. There are four vets here, and we're all women, so I hope you'll understand." She was apologizing! Huh? So Dad says to her, "We're simply glad you're here. Why does being all women have anything to do with being a good clinic?" And she says, "Well, in this area, some folks aren't real comfortable having women . . ."

Then you should have heard Mom interrupt. "You know, some folks out here ought to be shot!" She didn't mean that, really, but Mom was still very upset, and everyone knew it was only an expression. And then she said, "Why would someone shoot a dog? Does Bonner look like a deer or a raccoon or some other varmint that people like to shoot?" I've never seen Mom so upset. I think MnD are having culture shock, too.

There's also one unbelievably nice thing about the clinic that's different from Dr. Plank's old office. It's really cheap. They sell you any medication your pet needs at their cost. Plus, you don't pay for follow-up visits, like when Bonner gets his stitches removed. Dr. Tanners gave us this whole speech: "People won't come back if they have to pay again, but we have to monitor our patients, watch for infections and other problems. But folks figure, well, it's only an animal. Breaks our hearts seeing some of the neglect around here. We're doing what we can. We're educating people." Yeah, remedial education! So walking out, I checked out the whole waiting room full of people, and something in their faces made me see what Dr. Tanners meant.

MnD would have paid anything to keep Bonner alive. I just assume they have "anything" and a little left over.

From: ChaseR@eureka.org
To: buddy list #1
Date: 28 September 12:02 am
Subject: Corn Festival e-newsletter from Chase

Volume 1, No. 4 (I think)

* *

```
< ° \    EXCITING NEWS FROM OUR LOCAL CORN FESTIVAL
  /  \        THAT'S BEEN SITTING IN MY COMPUTER
 m  m           FOR WEEKS! SO IT'S OLD NEWS!
```

   / \   (This issue's mascot is the crow, and his friend the scarecrow, which looks more like a pumpkin head, I guess. Well, the pumpkin festival's coming up.)

* *

```
  _~\|/|~
_( + | + )~    Hey, everyone! This issue will be pretty short, but I
  ( ++0++ )        didn't want you to think I'd forgotten about you.
 ~/\|\\|/\\~       Mom and Dad and I went to the Millersburg Corn
```
Festival with Melissa's family (the Cogdons) and the Harris kids from Columbus, and my new guitar teacher sat with us for part of dinner. Next year everyone has to come out for it. I mean, it's really po-dunk, however you spell that. And tiny, but it's still packed with thousands of people. There's a midway—big whuptedoo—and cheesy rides for the tots, but they have the best corn in the solar system. They shuck the husk down so it makes a handle. And then they dunk the ear into a huge kettle of butter. So delicious. 25Ø.

(Sorry, I can't find the cents symbol!) White and yellow and the two-color kind. IncrEDIBLE. We didn't go to hear the barbershop quartet. (Might have reminded Mom that I haven't had my hair cut since we've moved.) And we didn't go for the morning parade, where all the local high schools send their marching bands to trample the little patch of grass in the town square. But we did see:

Event 1: Corn-spitting Contest. Yup! They use canned corn for this. (No, not creamed corn.) But anyone can step right up (I DID!) and take a kernel, and give a big old spitooey and see how far it goes. They've got lines drawn on the ground. You get three tries. My best landed about four feet. The guy who won spit his corn a distance of six feet, one inch. I know that's not very far (that's how tall my Dad is), but you should try it sometime. Corn don't fly!

Event 2: Corn-eating Contest. Mom didn't let me enter this because it was going to be a waste of money (you had to donate $25 to the Moose Lodge) and lots of giant men had already entered. You get ten minutes to scarf down as many ears as you can. The corn's already shucked and cooked, so all you have to do is go typewritering along with your teeth right down the rows. You can't leave more than ten kernels on a cob or the judges make you go back and clean the ear. Talk about a disgusting mess: corn sprays everywhere, the kernels look like warts all over their faces, and the guys snort like pigs chomping it all down. Pretty gross. When it was over, the table DID look like dumped cans of creamed corn. The winner, Al Somebody from Straitsville, munched down 24 ears. We didn't stay for the women's contest. Oh, the winners each received $100, terrible stomach cramps, AND their photograph in the BEAVER CREEK BARFING.

Event 3: The Crowning of Little Miss Silver Queen. You know, with all these festival queens and princesses out here, I could end up marrying royalty one day.

★　　　★　　　★　　　★　　　★　　　★　　　★　　　★　　　★

In our not-so-exciting NEXT ISSUE:

> Nifty study tips from Miss Dummery, my guidance counselor

> Whatever else I think up

> And the answer to Today's Quiz Question:

> Q: If Columbus were to have a festival and crown a king and queen, what would the festival celebrate? (The rib festival by the riverfront can't count, even though it might be fun to see Little Miss Spare Rib and Big Baby Barbecue.)

Send your nominations to me and, while you're at it, to the Chamber of Commerce.

Bye for now,

Chase

q:¬(giant belly)<
(If I had entered the corn-eating contest!)

From: ChaseR@eureka.org
To: badaddtude@hottmailer.com
Date: 30 September 3:57pm
Subject: Greetings from < : 3   ) ~ ~ ~ ~ House

−Õ∫Ô−

You asked about Bonner, and I meant to write sooner just to say
he's healed pretty well. Thanks for asking. You were the only friend
I told, for now. (I haven't really been writing much at all with
school starting, orientation, and all.) Bonner has swelling where
the muscle's bruised, but it's smaller and he's acting as though it
doesn't bother him.

School is school. It's actually a lot like back in Columbus, except I
have to keep asking kids' names and introducing myself over and
over. I'm getting to hate the sound of my name I say it so much.
(Sometimes I say: "Chase, it's short for Chastity.") But I promised
my parents I would MAKE AN EFFORT, and it's not like I want to
spend all my time with no friends here. I mean, I know kids, and
I've done stuff with kids, like Aaron, Jeff, Sean, and Sam, etc. We
have a newspaper that comes out every month, so I joined that for
after school. If nothing else, I can just do my speedy typing for the
paper. We have tons of computers everywhere, but they don't teach
typing here. It's hunt and peck—and since kids already know how
to HUNT, it's only peck they have to learn.

But one thing's happened, I don't know if the shooting just got me
focused on this or what, but every day, ten, twenty times a day, I
think about dead things and killing and hunting. First off, there

62

are dozens of roadkills. Possums, deer, raccoons, cats, groundhogs, skunks, squirrels. Some roads you really have to dodge them. When I'm on my bike, there's no dodging the smell. Or how sickening they look up close.

The other part, like I said, is hunting. I never even thought about hunting—have you? ever in your whole life? But out in the country, everything says it. Maybe it started with all the cicadas dying. I don't mean to sound morbid. But I stare out my bedroom window, and I see how the moles keep making tunnels under the grass. You can see their whole network because they lift up the grass and it burns and dies, so there are these brown loops and lines scribbled in the green like they're making monograms in the lawn to show it's THEIRS. And I have to mow the lawn, and the wheels shred up the grass where the tunnels are. You can feel the tunnels under your feet. So I try to stomp the grass back in place. We all do, whenever we go across the yard. We're not trying to squash the moles, just the tunnels. They share 90 acres with us: can't they spare the little bit of lawn we have and burrow elsewhere? So either we get rid of them or give up the lawn. I think we're going to give up the lawn, though there are ads in the paper for Rid-a-Mole with pictures of dead moles with X's for eyes. HELLO! Moles don't really even have eyes! See fig. 1.

$$< \ 3 \ ) \sim \sim \sim \sim$$
fig. 1

They're not half the problem the mice are. I can't believe we're doing this, but we're X-terminating them. Everyone in the country has mice, and they're everywhere, and there's no trapping them in those little humane traps we used to set so you can drive the mice somewhere in the country to be free. WE'RE THE PLACE YOU DRIVE THEM TO! Plus, there are too many of them, and they destroy everything. (I know, the mice are only doing what mice do.) And they're in places you'd never expect them. Get this: So far, in addition to eating Dad's bran flakes, garlic cloves, saltines, and the dried corn we had hanging on the wall, the mice love the dogs' kibble. We've found piles of Nature Dog, Active Formula:

< : 3) ~~~~ in my rubber boots (surprise!)

< : 3) ~~~~ in the linen closet between blankets

< : 3) ~~~~ under the bedspread in the guest room (Sleep tight, don't let the bedmice bite.)

< : 3) ~~~~ in the pink roll of unused insulation in the basement

< : 3) ~~~~ in my backpack (hey, great trail mix!)

< : 3) ~~~~ everywhere

< : 3) ~~~~ everywhere else

But wait, that's not all. Remember, all this has happened in the four months since we've moved here. The mice have made nests (using the pink insulation among other things):

< : 3) ~~~~ in the stuffing of a lounge chair

< : 3) ~~~~ inside the Styrofoam box of my computer printer

64

< : 3   ) ~~~~ in the tractor's engine ($490 repair from Sears)

< : 3   ) ~~~~ in the air filter of the car (at first we thought we would ignore the ones in the garage, but it's too expensive)

Mice have also chewed:

< : 3   ) ~~~~ the wires of my headphones

< : 3   ) ~~~~ the phone cord stapled along the floorboards (before we got here)

< : 3   ) ~~~~ the carpet padding under the living-room rugs (before we got here)

< : 3   ) ~~~~ the edge of the couch I helped Dad reupholster

< : 3   ) ~~~~ two of my mother's wool jackets in the cedar closet

and, and, and, that says nothing about mouse shit on the shelves, in the back of drawers, in the closets, and and and and and and . . . and, more tonight. Got to run!

From: ChaseR@eureka.org
To: badadditude@hottmailer.com
Date: 30 September 7:07pm
Subject: Greetings from < : 3) ~~~~ House2

–õ∫Ô–

So we bought traps and hid poison where the dogs can't reach it, and every day someone (meaning: ME) has to check the traps and flush the dead ones down the toilet. The whole thing's creeping me out, lifting that metal bar from their crushed heads with the bulging-out eyes. Really nasty. But no choice. Dad's pushing steel wool in every nook and crack he can find in the basement and outside along the window wells. That's supposed to keep them out. Maybe things should get better. But for now, it's the worst.

I'm not going to go into it all. Maybe I'll devote my next e-newsletter to spiders. / \o/ \ Our windows feature the webbed-up all-you-can-eat insect buffet of wings and bees and flies. There are enough webs that we could just take down the window screens.

Time to crank out some reading for English class. Poetry. Thankfully we don't have to write any. Not yet. I'll write back tomorrow.

Chastity

P.S. Wait, I'm feeling a poem coming on . . .

P.P.S. Yes, yes, it's coming . . .

66

SPIDERS

Little Chase Riley

who looks like a smiley q : ¬)

was eating his jelly on rye, see?

When down came a spider

who sipped from his cider

Shoot! Can't think of an ending! Later!

From: ChaseR@eureka.org
To: badadditude@hottmailer.com
Date: 30 September 5:51pm
Subject: Our poem's exciting conclusion

And—look it!—he curled up and died. Gee.

Not a lot of good rhymes for "Riley." Oh, well. Later, Jeremy.

From: ChaseR@eureka.org
To: badadditude@hottmailer.com
Date: 1 October 3:21pm
Subject: Re: Re: Greetings from < : 3) ~~~~ House

–Õ¡Ô–

You're making me glad I'm NOT there taking more Latin. Mrs.
Leesburg was hard, but she doesn't sound anything like your new
teacher. Maybe he's got a toga wedgie up his butt. !Spanish is much
easier! except I can't find the keyboard-thing to make the upside-
down exclamation marks. But I just can't concentrate on it except
for ordering food at Taco Town, which is our only fast-food place for
miles. Thanks for the news, though.

Remember I was telling you about hunting? Well, just last night
this weird thing happened. Everyone at the general store is buying
hunting licenses and talking raccoons, and yesterday some guy
came to the front door around dusk with a truckload of dogs: a bas-
set hound and two official black-and-tan coonhounds and a beagle.
"Mind if I set up here for a few nights and help get rid of your coon
problem?" I told him we didn't have a coon problem and we don't
want anyone hunting on our land, which is how come Dad and I
stapled something like 200 fluorescent yellow WARNING! NO HUNTING,
NO TRESPASSING, GO AWAY WHOEVER YOU ARE THIS MEANS YOU, JERKO!
signs around our perimeter—but I guess he missed seeing those.

Well, this guy didn't believe me. "NO coon problem? Coons are
problems everywhere. Last owners begged me to come. THEY called

69

ME every year. Coons'll dig up your garden searching for grubs, rummage through the trash, eat the fish in the pond—generally make a huge mess of everything. Some's got rabies."

Bonner and Pirate were barking up a storm—they could smell his dogs in the truck, though his were being quiet. "How about you let me talk to your parents, young man," he says, so I go find Dad so Dad can tell him exactly what I told him.

The fact is, this guy's already unfolded his lawn chair next to his pickup like he planned to hunt whether we were home or not. So he explains to us, "See, I'll wait real quietlike there in my chair. And I let the dogs get on the scent—no use my running all around the property until they're on to one."

My dad did all the talking. "How do you know they've found one if you're up here?"

So the hunter says, "I just listen. When they take off together, they have one kind of barking, it's like a let's-see-what's-out-here yelping sort of talk. And then when they've found one, they switch to a hey-everyone-I-got-one-over-here bark. And then once they've treed a coon, the barking switches to we've-got-him-trapped-now-where's-that-guy-we-work-for howling sound. You get to know the difference. So that's when I go on over with my flashlight here and see what's what and take down the varmint."

I thought those different dog voices were pretty interesting. Maybe our dogs have those barks, too, since they're part hound. But I was mostly thinking, How come Dad isn't telling him to get the hell off our property? No, Dad just asks him how long it takes for the dogs to find the coons, and how many he can shoot in a night.

On a "good night" (good for him, not the coons), he says he bags three or four. He says, "Could start tonight, if you don't mind. The hounds are already excited."

Then my dad tells him no, we'll just leave the raccoons alone and risk whatever damage, and he thanks the guy for stopping by. And then the coon hunter looks at us like we were insane, like we had just told him we planned to sit by and watch our property be over-run by a squad of Godzillas with rabies. Now, if only this guy had known a way of siccing those dogs on cicadas, I'm sure we could have worked out a deal with him back in June.

What's wrong with people around here? Why does everyone want to shoot something? Not the girls—but the guys at school talk about it more than they talk about girls. Or sports or music. Here's what they shoot: wild turkeys, squirrels, doves, pheasants, grouse (not sure what those look like), coyote (as if!), deer, muskrats, coons, beaver, groundhogs, pop cans, bottles, lions, tigers, and bears, oh my.

Whatever. Bye now from the Pickway County Mouse House & Coon Preserve,

q:¬)   (That's not a coonskin cap.)

From: ChaseR@eureka.org
To: Melissa_cogdon@reachout.com
Date: 4 October 11:42pm
Subject: Haven't heard from you

Dear Melissa,

How's school going? I've heard from a few people and I guess
you're doing well. Seen any good movies? We have all these movie
channels because we have this satellite dish and no movie theaters
close by, so I've caught up on lots that I never got around to seeing
(never even wanted to see). I've also seen the DIE HARD sequels
and the TERMINATOR stuff too many times. And an old mummy
movie marathon.

$$(\backslash / : / \prod \backslash) \ | \ / \backslash \ (\backslash \backslash \ | \ / < \backslash \backslash \ | \ / \backslash \ | \ / / \ (\backslash \backslash / \backslash \ | \ [$$

My school's still pretty much like the old school, except most kids
have long bus rides coming from farther away in the county. Not
as many kids think about going to college here, so there's more
vocational stuff to take if you want. You wouldn't believe how
many kids drop out around eleventh grade so they can work on
the family farm or in construction or at the mill. I haven't met
anyone who wants to be an environmental engineer like you. I
can't even remember what that is . . . Kind of different. Definitely
feels like we don't belong, or perhaps it's just we can't or don't
want to, but there's no changing everybody else so they'll belong to
what we—never mind. See, I get all bogged down trying to figure
things out.

Your last e-mail was pretty funny. Can Leigh Anne and her sister actually carry a tune? Remember that time they were singing along to the radio, and you said they sounded like cats auditioning for a kitty litter commercial? I thought they'd scratch you to death.

Farm chores call.

q:¬.   ∞∞∞∞∞∞∞∞∞∞∞∞∞ (: :) ` ` ` ` (: :)

(That's me ignoring the call . . .)

From: ChaseR@eureka.org
To: badadditude@hottmailer.com
Date: 4 October 6:50am
Subject: New Shower

−õʃÔ−

I figured out the best thing about living out in the middle of no-where: showering outside. No. 1 Reason to Move to the Country. Dad and I finished installing this outdoor shower on the side of the house so we can hose off the dogs whenever they're stinko or so we can rinse off after working in the poison ivy or whatever. It's just a showerhead and faucets—no plastic stall or bathtub or anything like that. It's got small round gravel to stand on, and an old footlocker filled with towels, and then a row of pine trees on one side and the long view of the cornfield on the other side. At dawn today I went out and took a really long hot shower—as long as it took the sun to rise completely above the horizon—just standing there bucko naked with all this steam clouded around me. No one else was up. We don't have any neighbors anywhere close that could see. So great. Like being somewhere in the middle of nothing—in the middle of nature, I guess—just like people used to do before there were shower curtains and bottles of kiwi-and-vanilla-scented shampoo. Mallory can have the bathroom to herself when she's home. The outside shower's mine.

Off to school!
Nakedman
{ :¬)   :   · | 8⇒

From: ChaseR@eureka.org
To: riley79@kentstate.edu
Date: 4 October 6:50am
Subject: WAKE-UP CALL! for &8^/)

Hey, Mallory:

How'd your first midterms go? Harder than you thought? Did you get the Survival Kit that MnD sent? I picked out the butterscotch drops you like and the licorice stuff, and they added the vitamin C candy and those tins of instant coffee that smell like ice cream. You probably aced all your exams and got all your papers back with a little ☺ next to the A. Oh wait, that was elementary school. ☹

I actually got an A on something I did in school. Turns out me and Español are amigos. (I even figured out how to make the Spanish accent marks on the keyboard. ¡Olé!) And my other classes are OK. I'm not the brainiac you are. At least for now.

The dogs and me, and this other kid Aaron who races mountain bikes, we all walked around our whole property yesterday. Takes about an hour and a half. Aaron lives with his mom and his mom's mom in the house where they were all born. Three generations in one house. Anyway, some of the plastic NO HUNTING signs we put up are already gone. Ripped down from their staples. So Dad wants me to replace them.

I learned some things from Aaron I didn't understand. There are trees around our land with pieces of 2x4's nailed up one side. Maybe you knew, but they're deer stands that hunters use for hiding. They climb up those steps and make a little platform in the branches, covering up the sides with other branches and stuff. And then, real quietlike, they just drink beer until some deer comes along to eat the corn husks or lick the salt blocks they've just so happened to have dumped nearby. And then, KABLAM! Deer becomes venison.

Aaron hunts with his dad. He's got his own license, took a hunter education course they teach at the volunteer fire department, has a coat rack in his room made from deer antlers—ones that he's found just walking the woods. The more he told me, the less I liked him. I feel bad saying that, because he's nice enough. But I can't connect with Aaron, sort of the way I never connected with those guys at school who were SO into hockey. I like skating as much as anyone, but those guys did nothing but eat, sleep, drink, shop, talk hockey.

Am I making sense? I've met kids besides Aaron, like Jeff and Sean and his brother Sam, but I get the feeling everyone's already in a gang that's been together for years, long before I came to their school. I guess like I used to have in Columbus.

Hasta luego,

Señor Chase

q : ¬)

From: ChaseR@eureka.org
To: buddy list #1
Date: 4 October 11:42pm
Subject: 1 month of school down, 8 to go (then only 36 more until graduation!)

VOLUME I, NO. 5

**********COLLECTOR'S ISSUE*********

Hey, everyone! Welcome to the very late fifth issue of my e-newsletter, which I haven't finished but I figured I had to send anyway so I don't appear to be lost in cyberspace.

Today's feature story comes to us compliments of the BEAVER CREEP BEACON. This week's issue arrived with a four-page, four-color insert from Ohio Trading Co. (I don't know if you can TRADE anything, because everything in their ad costs plain-old dollars and cents.) "What is it?" you ask. Four pages of hunting gear!

So first, let's introduce our two opponents: deer v. deer hunter. And now let's see what each opponent brings to this great sport:

THE DEER 3 : ○ |

a. Powers: the five senses (with an extra keen nose), small brain, scared shitless personality, decent sprinting ability

b. Superpowers: none to speak of

c. Additional equipment: nope

77

THE DEER HUNTER [(; ¬ /)

a. Powers: the five senses, major brain (underused), fancy finger work

b. Superpowers:

1. Invisibility: "Try SCENT-BE-GONE, $6.99, which kills human scent on contact" so deer can't smell your presence, and the SILENT STALKER JACKET, $34.95, with camouflage pattern.

2. Extravision: "Try our long-range sighting scopes and binoculars." Prices vary from $24.99 to $279—at that price, you'd better be able to use them as x-ray specs, too!   (o) (o)

c. Additional equipment (see below)

Below:

Now here's a selection of the other items Ohio Trading's offering on special this week to make your hunt successful. Of course, they got your guns, with names like EXPRESS SUPERMAGNUM COMBO, $399.99. (What can you say except KKK—KASPLAT! KAPOW! KABOOM!) For you little kids, there's the EXCLUSIVE YOUTH MODEL SHOTGUN, $110.99. And a local favorite, none other than the SUPER-VALUE SAVAGE MODEL 64F for less than $100. ("Savage"? Who wants to be a savage? Maybe it's a typo for "Savings." Or "ravage"?)

Of course you'll need bullets—on sale this week. Some coincidence! How about a box of WINCLEANS, $12.99, that are "guaranteed to shoot clean."* (*The type's too small to read what the * means.)

Now to ensure perfect marksmanship, you'll want to bring the deer within point-blank range, right? "Try some STILL STEAMIN', $10.99, nature's most potent deer attractant!" (Guess what's "still steamin'"?) And GRUNT MASTER DEER CALL, $12.99, so you, too, can imitate a buck and woo all those lonely deer over for lunch. YOUR lunch. OK, everybody, tell me why this is called a sport. Maybe I should make that Today's Quiz Question. All right, I will.

Today's Quiz Question: Why?

I thought I had more time to work on this issue, but I made a few promises to my folks about improving grades and concentrating on homework and—MOM! I'll be right down, promise, I'm signing off this instant!—I got to go.

Being Chased

, ' , ' , ' , ɋ : ¬ /   (me running, the sweat pouring off)

But still time to paste in:

* *

CRIMES OF THE COUNTRYSIDE

>>>>>Beaver Creek, September 28. County Sheriff's Office responded to a Main Street address on a report of a domestic dispute that reportedly started over who could use a video game controller first.

>>>>>Jersey, September 28. A woman at the Econo Truck Stop reported that a man was cutting counterfeit money out of sheets of paper. Police found the man, who said he was just

playing a joke. Police took away his copies [and then bought a bunch of doughnuts for the road].

*　　*　　*　　*　　*　　*　　*　　*　　*

In our NEXT ISSUE:

> Culinary highlights from the Beaver Creek High School cafeteria (Seriously great peanut butter cookies) C=:¬b

> Shopping ideas from Sweeney's General Store (items you haven't been able to find anywhere for years, they still stock here. Sure, the packages are a bit faded, but they come with price stickers from the 1990s! Quantities are limited—like one or two of each—but these babies are priced to move!)

> And the answer to Today's Quiz Question:

Bonus Q: What do the four "H's" in 4-H stand for?

All items reprinted from the BEAVER CROOK BEACON are true.

> – " , " , " , " – { o >

Nothing fishy about anything reported here! Promise.

From: ChaseR@eureka.org
To: badadditude@hottmailer.com
Date: 5 October 10:19pm
Subject: Good-bye, Cruel World

Dear −Õ∫Ô−

You are SO right. I vow not to turn into another Celia Lockowitz. I didn't really think she was that weird, but she shouldn't have always brought up all her cruelty-free products in every single class—like in chorale.

So thanks for the big advice. I'd love to "get over it." DUH. I just can't help myself. Shooting, killing, roadkills, even flocks of killdeer—it's inescapable. Get this: We had an all-school hunting safety assembly today. (I could have done the lecture in two words: DON'T FIRE. Any questions, class? OK, we're all safe then.) People don't think the way we did in the city. It's crazy. These kids will be talking about getting some new Buckmaster crossbow at lunch, and so either I just listen—which means they'll just assume I'm all into it, too, and can't wait to get my own—or I change the subject and they look at me like I'm from that other planet . . . Columbus. Light-years, Jeremy. Maybe it IS just a time warp.

This last weekend a pond expert came over. This was pretty cool. We wanted advice on controlling the algae, but immediately he goes into why we need to pull up the cattails. Why? Because we need to eradicate (his word) the muskrats or they'll end up ruining the dam and burrowing through the pond's clay lining. He gave us the names of a couple of guys who specialize in sending muskrats to kingdom come. (Beavers are even worse for ponds supposedly.) See? Every day someone brings up something to kill. So I start to forget about one thing, and then instantly there's something else to get over. I guess bats are the only animals we're supposed to want, but Mom is terrified of bats. Oh, and Dad's terrified of snakes, even though, it turns out, we don't have a single poisonous species around here. (Gee? Maybe they might have thought about all this before uprooting our lives in Columbus.)

But what I'm trying to say is, I look over at Bonner, who really has healed, and I'm reminded how whacked out some people can be, and I think his being alive will always always always remind me of that. (Don't you hate how spell check automatically underlines everything like repeated <u>words words words words</u>?)

Speaking of experts, Mom talked to the guidance counselor Miss Dummery (perfect name) because they're concerned about their son's Introverted Personality, meaning me, meaning how come I haven't made nineteen special best friends since moving here and how come I spend so much time on the computer and how come I seem so moody (never mind that my dog was shot the first summer we moved here) and how come I don't seem to enjoy spending time after school at some of the nice clubs the school sponsors. (I already am in the newspaper club, but that sounds too much like spending MORE TIME on the computer for them.) Was I introverted in Columbus? No. I was PERverted, right?

.

Here are Miss Dummery's suggestions to Mom.

- Chess Club—challenges the mind and it sure is fun. Take turns bringing in snacks for everyone.
- 4-H Club, where I can learn how to fatten up pigs and cows to sell to the slaughterhouse. ("Bye, bye, Pokey. I'll miss you.")
- The Beaver Creek Marching Band. Like I can play guitar in that?
- Art Club, where I can help create the bulletin boards in the hallways and even use glitter sticks and the staple gun—be extra careful!

How come? If I, Chase Riley himself, can't explain why, then how could dumb Miss Dummery know? I AM NOT spending one study period in her office pretending I have a Problem so I can talk to some lady who wears clothes with strawberry appliqués and doilies and laces like one of those concrete geese people put in their yards.

Jeremy, will you be one of my witnesses when I go wacko and hitchhike to Antarctica or Namibia and become a hermit crab? (What do hermit crabs eat? Don't tell me: cicadas.)

Bye from the Extracurricular Terrarium, Muskrat Refuge, and Counseling Center for UNtroubled Youth,

Chase

$\overset{\bullet}{|}$ q : ¬0   (Dummery knocking some sense into me with her baseball bat) (STRIKE ONE!)

From: ChaseR@eureka.org
To: riley79@kentstate.edu
Date: 17 October 5:19pm
Subject: More about Bonner. Brace yourself.

Dear Mall,

My last few e-mails were short (and yours were so short they didn't even bother to arrive), so you'll have to let me tell you more today. (Miss Dummery, my Guiding Light, also thinks that keeping a journal might help with My Transition, and she said that letters could count. Even e-mail. So Mom and Dad have relented and let me spend more time on the computer. Score one for the home team!)

I thought Bonner was going to mend perfectly and he did. OUTSIDE. No scar or anything. But something's gone wrong INSIDE. Inside his head. You know Thanksgiving starts deer season. Well, people are practicing up. The guns are so loud that even faraway shots sound very loud, like they're coming from right behind whatever tree or building you're near. During dinner someone nearby must be target shooting. There are rounds of gunfire and then nothing. And then more rounds and then nothing. Sometimes it lasts for hours, off and on. Bonner now goes crazy at the sound. Just panicking. Like a nervous attack. He trembles, rushes over to the closest person, tries to climb on your lap or under you—and nothing we do will calm him down. He pants and quivers and just shakes until the gunfire is over—until about fifteen minutes after the shots have stopped. I can only guess he thinks he's going to be shot again.

We had a pretty loud thunderstorm last night, and that must sound like shots, too, because he acted the same way, only for longer. I didn't sleep at all. He clawed under the covers, then out, and then back under. Trembling the whole time. I kept petting him and I stroked that spot on his belly that's supposed to be soothing, and I kept telling him, "You're all right" and "Nothing's going to hurt you." Pirate sort of snuggled next to me, too, just to get a little of the attention. The sound doesn't bother him.

I don't know what we're going to do. You should see his face, it's pitiful, like he's saying, "Protect me, they're coming for me—and for you, too!"

I figured you had to know.

I have a ton of homework (if I get around to doing it), and Dad expects help around here almost every night since he finished up one course and has a little time. There's always some repairing or hauling or cleaning. That's what it means to have a new OLD house. MnD still have to park outside since we've hardly touched the garage. Old Mr. Fitzweller sure was a pack rat. We're having our third garage sale the weekend before Thanksgiving.

I'm glad you wrote back. If I had another sister at college, you'd only have to write back half the time.

Holding down the fort,

Chase

q. ¬O   (Yawn, I can barely stay awake.)

From: ChaseR@eureka.org
To: badadditude@hottmailer.com
Date: 24 October 10:01pm
Subject: Bathtime

−õ∫ô−

The funniest thing happened yesterday. Not completely funny because Bonner was a wreck again as soon as the thunder began, but we had houseguests: some professor Dad met at a conference and her husband, whose specialty is tapeworms. Sandra Murakami, Dad's friend, is also a doctor, of something like epidemiology, which she explained wasn't only about plagues and epidemics. They're both Dr. Murakami, both about sixty, and both very polite and kind of stiff.

So before breakfast there's rumbling—the rain hadn't begun—and Bonner races over to me at the kitchen table, and I go eat my cereal on the floor and comfort him. But then there are more thunderclaps, and he bolts for the only place he feels safe and that's my bathtub, which is also the guest room bathtub. The door there doesn't really close right, and you have to pull it so it sticks shut—but it can't lock. Now picture this: Dr. Murakami (the wife) was inside bathing, but did that stop Bonnerboy in his panic? No way! He hurled himself at the door, shoved inside, and leaped into the tub. It didn't matter that the curtain was closed, that someone was bathing there, or that—SURPRISE!—the tub was full of water. All we heard was this horrified scream (just like in that PSYCHO movie!). Then this loud splash.

Dad, Mom, the other Dr. Murakami, me, Pirate—we all rushed over to see what had happened. The bathing doctor grabbed a nearby towel and floated it on the water to cover herself. Bonner was sitting in the tub, right next to the doctor, trembling, probably thinking, See? She's afraid of thunder, too.

I coaxed Bonner out of the room, and Mom apologized fifty hundred thousand times, explaining about Bonner's problem. Both Dr. Murakamis kept laughing all through breakfast.

But it turns out that the wife doctor knew about some medication Bonner should try. It's supposed to calm dogs during storms. We called the vet clinic and got some, and next time we know a storm is coming we're to give him a pill. It won't do any good if he's already trembling because the pill only relaxes him before his brain moves into this phobia state. That's what Dr. Murakami explained to us. See, Bonner gets all terrified even though nothing is going to hurt him, and that's phobic, she says, because it prevents him from doing normal things like sleeping or walking or anything. He won't even eat TABLE food when he gets panicked.

Only problem is, any time the forecast is for thunder, we have to slide a pill down his throat, and those reports are right maybe half the time—and who's going to forecast hunters? Not so easy. Any advice?

Got to run,

Chase

q : ¬)

From: ChaseR@eureka.org
To: buddy list #1
Date: 31 October 7:49pm
Subject: E-Newsletter is in the works

VOLUME I, NO. 5$\frac{1}{2}$ (This one can't count as a whole issue.)

Hey, everyone. I'm going to write everyone really soon, promise. But I've saved up some hot items from the BEAVER COOKED BACON's police reports, so I'll just send this in the meantime.

CRIMES OF THE COUNTRYSIDE

>>>>>Ridgely, October 17. Park officers confronted a boy who was reportedly shooting off a bazooka. The weapon was found to be a homemade potato gun. Officers confiscated the gun and advised the juvenile of the risks he'd taken.

>>>>>Doleville, October 21. The sheriff assisted a Mr. Owen Courtney, 72, who reported the theft of a dill pickle and a pint of cranberry juice. Total value: $1.25.

>>>>>Cliffside, October 21. A cleaning person at the Parkview Swimming Pool snack bar reported that a patron offered her some laughing gas. Police found the man and asked him to leave per the manager's request. [This is no laughing matter!]

>>>>>Inniswood, October 23. Police assisted the Millersburg Volunteer Fire Department with a DRIER fire at Bubbles Laundromat on Herbert Avenue. [Much harder to put out than a wetter fire in the DRYER, right?]

From: ChaseR@eureka.org
To: Sandra Murakami, PhD, MD <smurakami@nhmed.lab.edu>
Date: 31 October 7:50pm
Subject: Quick Question

Dear Dr. Murakami,

Thanks for leaving us your card with your e-mail address. I know you probably don't want teenagers writing you, even though you said I could, but I do have a question. First I meant to say it was great meeting you and your husband and I hope you'll visit again. Bonner won't stop talking about skinny-dipping with you. Are you still afraid of thunderstorms?

Here's my question: We can't really give Bonner the medicine you told us about. The gunshots and thunder really scare him now, but the pill makes him so sleepy he's barely conscious. He gets so out of it and won't wake up for hours. I don't think we can keep Bonner drugged up the whole fall while hunting's going on. If we take a walk and one shot rings out, it triggers something in Bonner's head, and he starts to sprint home with his tail between his legs, and then he's so petrified to be out in the open away from me that he runs back and tries to squeeze between my legs. This dog was never afraid of things before.

I know your specialty isn't really veterinary medicine, but you seemed to know a lot about this. Or do you know someone I can ask? I'd be really grateful if you did. We also might take Bonner to a specialist in Columbus.

My sister, Mallory, says I shouldn't go on and on with e-mail letters just because I can type 51 words a minute (my current record). Sometimes I think my mind types even faster than my hands, especially lately because it seems there are too many things to think about.

So I'll end by saying I hope you and the other doctor are doing well and that you'll have a chance to write back soon.

Happy Halloween!

Chase Riley

```
\             __          /
  \ (  0  0  )  /
     (    O   )
    (         )
   (           (
     )          )
        (      )
           \   /
            /
```

From: ChaseR@eureka.org
To: riley79@kentstate.edu
Date: 19 November 6:11pm
Subject: Bonnerboy

Dear Mall:

Thanks for the phone call but, listen, you don't have to. I know Mom called you to tell you to call me. Everyone in this family tells one person one thing they're not supposed to tell someone else, and then that person tells that someone anyway, so what's the point? I'm fine, like I said on the phone. I get out plenty. I go out when I want to, but I don't much want to right now. I just can't leave Bonner shaking and quivering. At least if I can help it. I can be home by 3:30 and Mom and Dad are never here before 6:00. And they're in bed before 10:00—I don't blame them or anything, since Dad still commutes almost an hour and Mom has to be at work by seven. Plus, this isn't going to last forever. Probably Bonner will learn that nothing's going to hurt him. Maybe he'll get used to the gunshots. Or maybe they'll just stop right after deer season, like around Christmas break when you'll be home. If I don't finish this essay on Steinbeck, I'll get another incomplete, so I'll send the other part of this letter later. Chase

P.S. Yes, we did try to make an appointment for Bonner with this vet hospital in Columbus. But Mom made the mistake of saying it wasn't an emergency, so it's not for three weeks. Hunting season'll be over. Or maybe not.

From: ChaseR@eureka.org
To: riley79@kentstate.edu
Date: 20 November 6:45am
Subject: Rise and shine!

Dear Mall:

Zzzz . . . Are three hours of sleep enough? Whatever. I finished the
essay, fell into bed, and, three hours later, there's Dad knocking at
the door at sunrise. You're right, we'll try giving Bonner half the
pill or maybe a quarter. Dr. Murakami's e-mail said the same
thing. (She also said to try not to be overly distressed at his distress,
because that signals to him that his fear's legitimate.) But that
would only work for thunder, not gunfire. We'll try anything
because we can't have Bonner just lying around almost uncon-
scious. The first time I thought he really was overdosed because he
just wouldn't wake up. We'd move him, he'd try to stand, but he
was too wobbly. He'd open his lids but then fall back asleep. He
ignored the doorbell. This medicine isn't right for him. And if we
gave it to him every time gunfire started, he'd be drugged out every
day except Sunday, since supposedly there's no hunting on Sunday.
(Dad says that's only because there are no Sunday beer sales.)
Thankfully, there's rarely shooting after dark, so I've been able to
sleep pretty much every night without Bonner clawing over on top
of me.

I've made MnD promise that we can drive to Columbus or
Pittsburgh OR ANYWHERE ELSE the first days of open hunting season when everybody from all over Ohio will be rushing out here to

shoot. I'm glad you like your dorm and your roommate and your classes and Kent State and the cafeteria food and everything else. You're just the kind of person who likes new things. I don't know if I am. Maybe one day. Is it bad to like things the way you used to like them? More later. I have something I want to tell you.

Chase

q : ¬]

From: ChaseR@eureka.org
To: riley79@kentstate.edu
Date: 20 November 5:00pm
Subject: We are the Nature Channel ®©™

Mallory,

Back from school and doing an interview for our newspaper about
Sean and Sam's great-grandfather, who just turned 100. He went to
Pickway Middle School in its first year. (Another building that was
torn down.) Also back from walking the dogs. Since we've moved
here, Mall, we've seen more and more deer. They're so beautiful and
they're bigger than I thought—it's not like seeing a chipmunk or a
little heron. It's not like watching the Nature Channel; it's like being
one. We see them everywhere—bounding through the cornfields,
drinking from the pond—everywhere except in the rhododendrons,
which is the only thing we really notice they're eating.

Bonner and Pirate find all the places they've been sleeping in the
woods. It's usually where the ground cover's trampled. You should
see the dogs with their noses trained to the ground, zipping back
and forth in the forest. Or they race side by side along the narrow
deer runs. And sure enough, they pee probably 30 or 40 times every
walk, just to show the deer that two big mean ferocious mad dogs
are protecting this place. Do you think the deer know that our land
is the one safe place for miles around? Everybody else, as far as I can
tell, hunts their land or let's someone else hunt it. The Randolphs
next door have signs everywhere, too, but they also have those deer
stands. "We have the signs because we don't want anyone ELSE

94

hunting our land," Jeff told me a few days ago when I asked. Jeff's in both my biology and my algebra class. Last night he and his dad dropped over. You know, next week's their big day. Big day for everyone around here. No, not Thanksgiving—that's just cook-up-a-< : >== day. But right after Thanksgiving is Thanks-for-deer-season Day, and that's the real celebration. Some kids even miss school Monday to go hunting, and the school counts that as an excused absence. (Try that in Columbus!) So the Randolphs wanted permission NOT to hunt our land, but—get this: "We want to know, if we do wound a deer and he comes onto your land, can we cross on over and pursue it so we can put it down right? You know, so it won't suffer."

So what does Dad say? I know, I know, some people wouldn't even have bothered to come over and ask. That WAS respectful of them. (Which didn't surprise me since Jeff is a really good student: nice to everyone, whiz-kid smart, quiet.) But what does Dad say? "Sure, all right, but maybe try not to shoot right next to our property so the deer ends up running onto our land. But if you have to, just do what you need to do quickly."

Was I supposed to stand there, like the hall lamp? So I add, "Wouldn't it be easier not to shoot them at all? Then there'd be no problem about coming on our land or about chasing wounded deer."

And with that—I promise, I was speaking politely, too—Dad tells me to take the dogs for a walk because they were pestering everyone. All they were doing was sniffing Jeff and his dad, who have four beagles. Or maybe five now.

Mallory, I hate this: We have six different neighbors that border our property, and I've seen deer stands or blinds made of cornstalks or burlap sheets on every one. Two places have cornfields, and they've baited the area with cornstalks, mounded them in a pile real close to where they'll be shooting. And suddenly there are salt licks everywhere. The BEACON is printing stories like, Don't forget it's free hunting licenses for any senior citizen (that's a great idea! Let's have a bunch of blind-as-a-bat golden-agers firing their rifles from their rockers!). Also a story about how everyone should wear bright orange when out walking. A story reminding everyone to always bring the deer to a station for tagging, and if you do take more than your limit, it's a bare-butt spanking in front of the judge with all your friends watching plus no more $5-off coupons at the Kleen-a-Car Wash! Ever, ever, ever!

People are just going to do what they want and what's there to stop them?

(M: I'm going to just continue writing because I can use part of this for my English assignment. We have to do a persuasive argument and show both sides. So keep reading.)

It's like the whole county—the whole state—is gearing up for the Great Deer War of the Century. And we're sitting right in the middle of it all like a Red Cross tent that no one is supposed to bomb. I know there are other people around who don't allow hunting. And I know, I know, I know that plenty of people say there are good hunters who respect the law, who respect the environment, and who respect life, and they get a bad name because of the bad hunters. But I don't know. Not sure respecting life can include ending it.

I did more reading on the Internet for this report, skimming articles that came up when I did a search with "deer" and "hunting" and "overpopulation" and "venison" and a bunch of other words. Almost everything one organization says is true another one says isn't. It's like pro-choicers and pro-lifers arguing about abortion. Pro-hunters tell you why they're right and then the people on the opposite side—they're like ecology people and humane societies and just concerned people—tell you why they're right. It got so confusing or maybe just plain contradictory I had to make a list. Look how one group just cancels out anything the other group says.

FOR hunting: They say hunters remove surplus deer so their growing numbers return to a smaller, healthier population. But then the AGAINST people say, Wrongo! The deer have their own internal population controls. When their numbers get to be too many, the females give birth to one, instead of two fawns, and most of their offspring are males, so that there will be fewer deer in the next year.

Or the FOR hunting people say that hunting's a part of man's animal instincts. It's natural. It's wrong to deny it. Hunting's also our right as taxpayers and citizens of this country! The AGAINST people just shout bullshit about this. Just because we come from ancestors who used to hunt doesn't mean anything. Does that mean we also need to start hanging around in trees and grunting because our ancestors did that, too?

Then the FOR people say it's better to shoot deer than to let these animals starve during the winter. But then the AGAINST people say that's all backward! When nature takes its course, stronger animals will survive and live to breed, and only the weaker ones will die, and while that's not a happy thing, it is the way life is supposed to work.

But then I found some really smart FOR hunting arguments that say hunters kill the weaker animals because those are the slower ones or the less able ones.

So I started believing that, and then the AGAINST people argue that all the hunters want are big males, since they have more meat and bigger antlers. And those animals are the ones who ought to live and produce the best offspring. And they point out that females are in charge of population control, so killing males doesn't do as much good.

See how hard this is to decipher? It goes on and on, Mallory, and on and on and on. (My Internet search found 63,000 sites for "deer hunting" and 81,900 for "venison." Just in case you were wondering, it also produced 219,000 for "reindeer," so all I can conclude is that Christmas is one thing that still outranks hunting.)

What's your vote? It's hard to honestly know what's right. Don't you just have to do what SEEMS right, FEELS right, like in your heart, and quit listening to all the other arguments? MnD are so tired when they come home at night that more talk about hunting is the last thing they want. I can forward some of the documents I downloaded if you're interested, but I'm guessing you're not since you have too much to read as it is.

On the practical side, I did buy orange bandannas for the dogs and also bells—they're big as sleigh bells—to hang on their collars. For the next few weeks, whenever we're outside, they're wearing that so no one can possibly mistake a dog for a deer. (I did think for a moment that with the bells they could be mistaken for reindeer—but then I realized no one's going to fire on Santa's helpers.)

So if it's war our neighbor hunters want, it's war they'll get. (Did I tell you someone's been tearing down the NO HUNTING signs we posted?) I have also been making other plans. A Big Plan (with a capital "B" and a capital "P"). Something besides playing jingle bells. However, considering the way our family works, I can't tell you or anyone else without everyone knowing. Just let's say, I've been feeling awfully thirsty lately.

Study hard and finish whatever you're doing, and come home as soon as you can. Wednesday's my last day of school. Tell me exactly when you're coming and we'll do something OUT OF HERE. If you're worrying about me, don't.

Chase

q: ¬shhh (me with secret)

From: ChaseR@eureka.org
To: riley79@kentstate.edu
Date: 21 November 11:12pm
Subject: Stinking News

Dear Dolly Llama (AKA Mallory),

Don't tell ME the deer are out of control! PEOPLE ARE OUT OF CONTROL. And don't tell ME dying one way or another way is the same thing! Starving or being killed by coyotes (if there are any left) is the part of nature that just has to be, but the hunters and the builders who take all the land is the UNnatural part.

I am NOT becoming a fanatic who thinks every deer is Bambi and ought to have its own little garden to frolic in forever. I happen to read things besides the BEACON. But even the boobs who write for them say that because of the mild winter that's been predicted, we'll have more deer than ever. The state parks are even planning a "selective culling," which means they're hiring sharpshooters to kill a bunch of the deer. So, yes, I know deer are overrunning Ohio— lots of states—but isn't it because we've built houses on almost every square foot of land they used to roam? Tell me something I don't know. Tell me who knows how to solve the problem without making bigger problems. Can you do that, college girl genius?

So don't lecture me about how I'm just some naïve kid who doesn't know diddlysquat. YOU come up with an answer. You're not even here enough to know what's what, let alone to care.

Later . . . OK, so I didn't send that yet, because I knew when I got to the end there, that I wasn't really mad at YOU, but at other people. I am still somewhat mad at you, Mall, because you're only four years older than me and that's not enough to act like three months of college can turn you into the Dalai Lama or something. (I know your e-mail wasn't really a lecture, but you actually sent me more than five sentences, and that's the closest you've come to yelling at me the way you used to at home.) So I'm dropping the subject with you. But my Big Plan has been in Full Swing. Even though it may not work, I'M DOING SOMETHING. Wish me luck. Wish the deer luck. I'm finally taking a stand, you could say, and that's all you have to know.

One more bit of news in two letters: PU! Pirate found a skunk today. We were just doodling around the trails and out walks what Pirate thought was merely a squirrel in a tuxedo, a squirrel just being way too cocky. (It wasn't bolting into the trees, for one thing!) So Pirate runs for it, and the rest of the story is an hour of tomato-juice baths. When Dad got home, he ran to the vet for some bottled treatment he saw in their display case that really did get out the smell. (Meanwhile, what does PU stand for? Nowhere I looked had a definition. Particularly Ugh? Powerful Ultrastench?)

I managed to keep Bonner from joining in, but he still stunk from just bumping against Pirate, and I really stunk and I think I still stink, or maybe it's just that my nostrils haven't recovered. Bye now!

Chase

q:¬)

P.U. I mean P.S. I have not lost my sense of humor. Found this yesterday in the BEACON for the CRIMES OF THE COUNTRYSIDE feature of my e-newsletter:

>>>>>Mount Lime, November 18. Police received a complaint of loud music coming from a Saunders Road address. Police reportedly knocked on the door for ten minutes before the homeowner came to the door to let her dogs out. She said she hadn't heard the knocking because of the music. [Talk about WOOFers.]

From: ChaseR@eureka.org
To: riley79@kentstate.edu
Date: 22 November 11:11pm
Subject: Re: You, isn't it always?

I don't know what Mom said to you exactly, but she doesn't know everything. I tell the parentals plenty, but they're not exactly home all the time, and they don't come to school, so they don't know and shouldn't speak for me. Really, school is fine. I like it as much as you're supposed to like school. My grades are mostly B's. I'm probably going to apply for assistant editor for the second half of the year on the school newspaper. I'm "indispensable" there, according to our adviser, Mr. Jenks. (Thank YOU, sir!) There's a gang of kids that I eat lunch with every day, so I'm not off by myself. I practice guitar lots. My new instructor thinks that if I practice, I could be extraordinarily unexceptional. I walk the dogs. It's just that with you gone, I get all of Mom's worrying and pestering. When Dad's home, we mostly do farm repairs or painting and stuff, so we mostly talk about spreading drop cloths and whether to use finishing nails or screws.

So I don't need you worrying about me, too. THE ONE THING I wish were different is Bonner. He's his old self when there's no gunfire, but when there's shooting—well, then I have to be with him. There's no one else. Ask <u>me</u> if you want to know about me.

Me

q:¬|

From: ChaseR@eureka.org
To: Bill Weaver bill_weaver@ohdept.wildlife.pickway.net
Date: 22 November 11:12pm
Subject: A question about deer

Dear Mr. Weaver,

You probably won't remember me, but you came to our farm a few months ago and gave us advice about discouraging deer. I have a follow-up question I hope you can answer. If people are hunting all around us but no one is hunting here, will the deer figure out they can be safe on our land? Will they decide to stay on our 90 acres all winter then? Would that mean they'd probably eat all of my mother's new favorite thing, which is rhododendrons? I don't know if you can answer these questions, but thanks for trying.

Sincerely,

Chase Riley

From: ChaseR@eureka.org
To: badadditude@hottmailer.com
Date: 22 November 11:13pm
Subject: My Tea Party

Dear Jeremy,

You were right, that diet iced tea mix really does make you have to pee. Mom was pretty suspicious, because I never used to drink the stuff when she made a pitcher, but I told her that in human ecology we learned that most teenagers don't get enough fluids, so she's dropped it. I'm drinking like two quarts when I wake up, and even more after school. I've been taking the reindeer on real short walks, then putting them in the barn and picking them up after I've made my rounds. Even with orange bandannas and bells, I'm not letting the dogs anywhere near the property lines.

I've only seen one person the whole time. Most people hunt real early or around dark. (So says the wildlife office expert.) I move in, do my Business, tear out of there. The one guy I saw was Jeff's dad, Mr. Randolph, hanging this gauzy shower curtain around his deer stand. It's like 50 feet from our property. I waved to him, since I figured I was supposed to be quiet. Anyway, he called good morning to me, so I guess he wasn't trying to be quiet. Little did he know that the deer just might not be all that interested in the corn he's piled there for them—it's just not in the Big Plan for this season.

I've also managed to carry a hammer in my pocket and hide it under my sweatshirt. I've pried off the steps on, maybe, six tree trunks on the other bordering properties. So maybe the sides are getting a little more even around these here parts.

I was just rereading your last e-mail. You asked about other girls and the answer to your question is two. Well, Melissa stopped writing me back. She was only a friend, I guess, but since she was next door, she was cool. There's one girl in my study hall that I know wants to do stuff because she's been having people pass me notes all the time, and then there's also Marylynne Ross I mentioned before (or have I?), who's probably the closest to my age around where we live (all the properties that touch ours, except for the Randolphs', I think, are owned by people without kids or by people who don't live here but just farm the land or keep it for hunting). When the weather's too lousy for riding bikes, Marylynne and I sometimes carpool to school. So we're in-school and out-of-school friends. She's the oldest at home (her parents are separated) so she has to do almost everything around the house for her little sister and her father. She's pretty, prettier than most girls in school, but she doesn't have any time left for anything. And she doesn't have a computer for e-mailing. Sometimes I wish I didn't. That's when I wish I were a dog and could just sleep most of the day or growl at strangers. Write back soon.

Chase

q:¬Grrrrr

From: ChaseR@eureka.org
To: riley79@kentstate.edu
Date: 23 November 8:50pm
Subject: Re: What are you up to?

Wow, you're truly worried about me! Well, don't be. I'm fine. But I'm not discussing my Plan with you and that's that. I'm not up to no good. I'm up to good, and that's even more than I meant to tell you.

So, Mall, thanks for the e-mail. Did you get stood up or something and actually have another free moment to write to your brother?

From: ChaseR@eureka.org
To: badadditude@hottmailer.com
Date: 23 November 8:50pm
Subject: KABLAM

Dear Jeremy:

This morning in the BEACON, they had a chart of all the counties around here. Beneath each they listed how many deer had been killed last hunting season. In our county alone, which isn't that big, the number will be close to 6,000—6,000 dead deer! So how many of those deer will come from this township? How many from right around our house? And how many rounds of ammunition are going to be fired to kill them? Bonner's going to lose his mind with all the gunshots. Or he would have, if I hadn't started my "discouragements." Really, the only question is, how come there are so many goddamn deer and so many goddamn people?

It turns out our general store is one of the checkpoints. Hunters get these tags, and once they've killed a deer, they have to put a tag on its ear, and then take it to the checkpoint and register it, and when they've used their tags, their personal hunting season is over. Nearly every day now there's a deer lashed to a car roof or lying in some truck bed. The store's always got hunters in it, buying chewing tobacco and coffee (Dad says their coffee tastes the same as the chewing tobacco). I hear some of the men asking for directions, so even though I don't recognize everyone who's local, I know these guys are just here for the deer.

108

It doesn't make me go nuts shaking and acting nervous like Bonner, but I can't seem to focus on my homework. BLAM! right out of nowhere, a gunshot, like someone slamming a door when you're not expecting it. Try studying through that. They're not as loud as fireworks—no one's firing on our property, I don't think— but I can hardly concentrate. It's quiet, I'm reading, and then KABLAM, and I've jumped out of the chair. And Bonner's jumped into it!

And at the same time, I keep picturing some deer taking an arrow or a bullet right in the leg or the chest and running and bleeding across the floor of the forest, collapsing in a heap, and then some man dragging it by its rack half a mile back to the truck. Sorry, I know that's grim, but I keep seeing things like this even though I don't want to and I try not to. I turn up the music to keep from hearing the gunfire (then MnD tell me to turn it down). (Then I tell them to go away, but my volume's turned way down, too.)

Maybe Bonner imagines things, too, but with his own body getting hurt again instead of a deer's. I don't know. Try having breakfast to the tune of something being shot. It makes me nauseated. Plus, guzzling all that tea makes me pretty full.

Jeremy, it's weird, but is it possible I'm getting a phobia, too, like Bonner? It's just that all this hunting and shooting stuff is keeping me from doing what I need to do and that is how that one Dr. Murakami explained it. What am I supposed to do? Get our family doctor (like we've even got one out here) to prescribe me the human dosage of Bonner's pill and zonk out for the whole hunting season in bed? That would be easier, wouldn't it? In a way, that's what my mom and dad have been saying. "It's nice that you're concerned about the deer, Chase, and, of course, we're all heartsick about Bonner's panic attacks, but this is all part of life. Just get out more and enjoy things." So what am I supposed to say? How about: "Well, folks, you're never home to drive me anywhere I want to go where there might be kids to hang out with. Or should I just hang out at the post office, where all the old people come on account of the highlight of their day is getting mail from their grandchildren—that is, if they write!"

Find out more about your Thanksgiving plans and then let me know, and I'll try to find a way to hook up. You're so right: If MnD could have waited a year and a half, I could drive myself back and forth to Columbus. Mallory's car has just been sitting here the last three months.

Later,

Chase

q : ¬)

From: ChaseR@eureka.org
To: badadditude@hottmailer.com
Date: 24 November 8:02am
Subject: I don't know why I need to ask, but I do

Jeremy −Õ∫Ô−

I was up kind of early and reread my last e-mail to you, and then wrote you a letter, but I put it in the "send later" part, and I'm going to send you this one first. I just had this feeling that maybe I shouldn't be writing you all this, and that you're just doing me a favor reading it all and replying. (And I know your replies are short because you can't type very well, I understand.) But I don't know who else to tell. If you were sitting here I probably wouldn't say all this. But just typing and then hitting "send" seems different. Maybe it's too easy and I shouldn't bore you. Does this bore you? You're my best friend, so tell me before I bore you with any more letters.

I trust you to tell me, really.

Chase

q : ¬)

P.S. Practice your typing! Let's start with the home keys:

fdsa jkl;   fdsa jkl;   fdsa jkl;   fdsa jkl;   fdsa jkl;   fdsa jkl;
and don't stop until you fill the entire screen.

111

From: ChaseR@eureka.org
To: badadditude@hottmailer.com
Date: 24 November 6:50pm
Subject: THANKS! More BORING STUFF ahead!

–õĵÔ–

Forget I even wrote that last letter. I guess I just haven't seen you in a while, and Mallory and my parents keep saying I shouldn't write so much (but Miss Dummery keeps saying write MORE), and I just half thought maybe you thought so, too. Never mind! I'm back at the machine and cranking away . . .

I did this interview of this 100-year-old guy from around here. Pretty amazing what he could remember, since I can't even remember what I did last summer or how to spell the word "bulletin." (I have to look it up every time for my e-newsletter because you pronounce it "bulliten," right? Wait, I just saw the word "bullet" in it, and now I won't be able to forget.) One funny thing this guy told me: For several years (it was in the 1940s or something, I can't remember!), he won this contest where guys drop their drawers and sit bare butt on a block of ice and see who can stay there the longest. He won some other honors, too, like in WWI, but they weren't funny. When the article comes out in the school paper, I'll send it to you. It doesn't have the part about the ice-sitting contest.

112

From: ChaseR@eureka.org
To: riley79@kentstate.edu
Date: 24 November 10:44pm
Subject: Not so great news

Mallorina,

You know, I knew this would happen, because they're always in the road: Mom hit a deer tonight coming home. She didn't hurt it—at least it ran off after she hit it, or bumped it, maybe. And it didn't really damage the car except for one headlight, which the deer probably kicked. But Mom was really rattled. The deer had been standing in the road as she rounded this bend. And it froze there. It wouldn't move or anything, even though Dad had mounted these deer whistles on both cars that have this high-pitched whistle we can't hear but is supposed to warn deer that we're coming. So Mom slammed on the brakes and turned off her lights—but it was too dark to keep them off. When she clicked the lights back on, the deer had moved enough to prevent a real collision. Isn't that weird, though, how a deer acts paralyzed by your headlights, and even though it can run or jump out of the way, something inside it short-circuits or shuts off. It's something unexplainable, same as Bonner's phobia.

So Mom was alone and totally upset when she hit the deer. At first I didn't understand how upset she was. MnD came in my room to talk just about when I was checking e-mail. And Dad says, "Chase, son—" (you know that means we're getting Very Serious). And he says we (that means ME) need to get a little perspective on Bonner and the gunfire and this hunting situation on account of it seems like I've made it into my personal problem. "We're worried," he says, and Mom nods. Nowadays "We're worried" translates into "I'm wrong and they're right" about something.

So Dad points out how there was just as much hunting before we moved to the country as there is now, except now we're seeing it close up. So his suggestion is that I just try to ignore it just as I ignored it all when I lived in Columbus.

Then it was Mom's turn, and she said the usual stuff about how we just go on with our lives, lots of new things to handle since moving, etc., etc. "And as for the deer problem," she says, "let's leave that to the experts." So I tried not to scream when I said, "What experts? The expert who shot Bonner? No one around here cares. Back in Columbus people would have cared. Who did we know that hunted? NO ONE. Who had to wear bright orange just to walk around in the yard? NO ONE. Who would sit by and listen while 6,000 deer who have no place to go because of us—"

And Mom just blurted out, "Are you quite finished?" So, since I wasn't, I shouted right back, "No, you're interrupting me." And that brought our "discussion" to a close because I upset Mom and she left the room crying. And so Dad left to comfort her, but not before doing that look where he grits his teeth and shakes his head as if every problem in the universe were my fault.

I wasn't trying to upset anyone. But they can't just act like we live in Columbus. I'm just asking for a few answers and no one has them, and that makes people mad, because people, particularly our parents, want to HAVE ALL THE ANSWERS. And I write e-mails to you and to Jeremy, and you guys write back and that's great, but I know you can't understand what it's like to be here. And the county extension guy—I've been writing to him and talking to kids at school and to Mr. Sweeney at the general store . . . they all say, "Well, it's a messy situation, but you can't escape the fact that there are too many deer and they're going to starve if some aren't hunted, and isn't that worse?"

Mallory, you're taking that psychology class, so let me ask you this: Just because something can be worse, does that make something that's terrible any better? That's the thing I can't stop thinking. Well, I can stop, but once I get started, it's kind of like getting lost: even if you want to get home fast, you're still far away and have to find your way back.

I really do have other things to report, but you've probably already had to hit "page down" more times than you like. Oh, one quick thing: Jeremy says to remind you to bring home a large "Stolen from the KSU Athletic Dept." sweatshirt that he wants. Thanks. He'll pay you for it for sure.

See you soon! And don't be mad at me for writing.

ChaseR

q:¬)

From: ChaseR@eureka.org
To: badadditude@hottmailer.com
Date: 24 November 10:44pm
Subject: Stolen Shirt

Hey you −ÕʃÔ−

Thanks for forwarding Doughnut's new e-mail address.

I wrote Mallory about your sweatshirt. We'll see if she remembers. I almost told her I wanted one in fluorescent orange for hunting season, but I know they don't come in that color. And I guess that's especially not funny because Mallory told me Kent State is really sensitive about that 1971 shooting when the National Guard ended up killing those four students who were protesting against the Vietnam War. So I figured being funny wasn't going to be funny.

(That's using Good Judgment, Chase! Thank you, Dad.)

So where's your brother applying to college? I still think OSU would be great especially if we could room together and your parents don't make you live at home.

Mine would have . . . but our home is out here! Signing off. I have to watch some PBS special for English. I forget what it's called. Something with British accents and servants mumbling things like, "At once, Madam," and "Mahsta Chase will be taking his tea in the Hunt Room."

Chase

q:¬)

From: ChaseR@eureka.org
To: melissa_cogdon@reachout.com (/ °⌐°\ )
Date: 25 November 3:33pm
Subject: FW: Have Yourself a Very Vegie Christmas or Whenever

Dear Melissa:

My e-mail from two days ago came back from you saying "no such address." HUH? You aren't the one that moved! So I'm sending it again. Maybe your server was down. Maybe it's too late for this year, but here it is again.

Hey, Melissa:

I did get your e-mail so I did a quick Internet search and found you the address. They can express-mail this vegie turkey, but do it today or else it costs even more. Truthfully, it's not as bad as it sounds. It's like vegie bacon and vegie burgers: that textured soybean stuff like tofu and seitan (which is Japanese for SATAN, I think). And it tastes OK, not exactly like real turkey, but who cares? I guess you remember me talking about ours two years ago. That was when Mallory didn't eat any meat her junior year. I mean, we didn't eat that much meat anyway, but we all were trying to Respect Her Wishes. We still don't eat much meat, but we are having real turkey for this Thanksgiving. Someone down the road raises free-range turkeys and smokes them for the holidays. Mom called in an order. Sometimes I think we really have to give up anything that has to do with eating or wearing animals, and then other times I think I just can't think of everything right now.

117

Later, maybe. A little thinking now and then more later. I guess that's wishy-washy.

Anyway, Mallory convinced Mom to order this vegie turkey. It was like 15 pounds, I think, and it cost more than 50 pounds of real turkey, Mom pointed out. When it arrived, no one was very excited about giving thanks for tofu. But it really did look like a turkey. It was stuffed, plump, and round. The pretend skin even had little dimples on it. And it smelled good even raw, so people got more excited about dinner again.

So we're all at the table, and Mom's fixed all the usual great things, and my Aunt Tara and her three kids are over and so are both sets of grandparents, and here comes Mom—ta-ta-dah!— with the centerpiece: the turkey. Everyone gasps, "OOH!," all at once. But not the good kind of "ooh," the bad kind. And then I say, "No one said anything about eating a turtle for Thanksgiving!" It honestly looked like a huge turtle on a platter. The whole shape had collapsed into a flat mound that was even colored with tortoiseshell splotches. Dad pretended to carve it—but it fell apart. It tasted fine. We finished it. So if you order it, just prepare everybody for the turtle surprise. Maybe carve it up first.

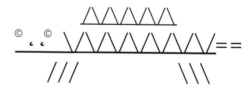

(Not such a great turtle. I need more symbols on the keyboard!)

Nothing's new otherwise. School's sort of easy. I guess it would be hard if I was really Applying Myself. You're probably scoring perfect A's as usual. I wish I were there to distract you in class.

Happy Pre-Thanksgiving, your Post-Columbus Friend,

Chase

q:¬) >==   (me with that gobbler thing)

From: ChaseR@eureka.org
To: badadditude@hottmailer.com
Date: 26 November 10:05am
Subject: Talk about Freezer Burn

Dear Jeremy −Õ∫Ô−

First morning of vacation, I went over to Jeff Randolph's. Mallory
ended up giving rides to a bunch of Columbus kids, so she came
late. Remember, Jeff's the kid in algebra with me and Jeff is a whiz.
We are talking, a MATHtermind! Jeff →　π[x-y]°9.2%(:7o)

He's taking algebra and trig at the same time—a few times he's
come over to help me with assignments. But I biked over there
today, and at one point I ran down to their basement to use the
bathroom because one of the other kids was bathing in the one
upstairs, and I see this ice-cream freezer, the kind they have at
stores where you slide the glass across the top and reach in for ice-
cream sandwiches and stuff. (His mom bought it at a tag sale.) So
I open it, just because, I don't know, it was strange to see this
freezer with pictures of ice-cream bars and frozen treats in someone's house. The only things in it were these brown-paper bundles
labeled: Stew, sausage, steak, ground, roast.

I went back upstairs and asked Jeff about it. "It's all deer meat. We
pretty much eat deer year-round," he says. "Mom's always cooking
up something with it. Breakfast sausage or lunch sandwiches or,
like, for dinner a casserole or pork and beans but with venison
instead. Once in a while there's other stuff, but the deer we get free

120

since we shoot it ourselves, and last year we were lucky and got some from my uncle who doesn't really like the taste." I guess I didn't realize it, but Jeff's family doesn't have much money. His father ran the service department at some car dealership, but he had to take early retirement because of some injury (I can't tell what it is or was), and now he has all these part-time jobs, so he's sometimes working night shifts and sometimes out-of-town jobs. Jeff's the oldest and there are five more kids—two from his dad's first marriage that live with them weekends. Deer is like their daily bread.

Jeff's mom offered us snacks while we were studying, but I just said no thanks since we're having a Thanksgiving dinner around three. All I could think of was some kind of deer snack, and I couldn't put that in my mouth. I did smell turkey cooking. Probably wild turkey, since there are lots of those around to shoot. I could tell I hurt Jeff's feelings when I said no thanks. He went back into the kitchen and came out with a bowl of pumpkin seeds that they'd roasted from pumpkins Jeff grew. They tasted great, and I said so, and then, when I left to go home, he gave me a sandwich bag filled with more.

I biked home the long way, past the houses that I always pass going home. But looking at their yards, I think something sunk in for the first time: Lots of our neighbors are probably hungry. I mean, the driveways were full of cars and lights inside showed people gathered at tables and all that. But I just understood it suddenly, how much the families around us are struggling, and everything proved it: the numbers that had almost worn off the mailboxes, and the two bicycles tipped over on the lawn that have been lying in the same position for months, and the volleyball net with clothespins holding up bunches of those pajamas that have feet in them. An old boat trailer with FOR SALE spray-painted on a big antifreeze jug. Nothing that I hadn't seen before, but all of a sudden I like really SEE it all. Mallory, who got an A on her freshman psychology midterm, would say it's because I suddenly stopped obsessing about me me me and Bonner Bonner Bonner and realized that other people have hardships, too—some that are a whole lot harder. That's the sort of stuff she writes in her e-mails to me.

But I do think about other people. I had just never thought about THESE people, I guess. Never really pictured how they were raising their families with deer meat and pumpkin seeds and way too little, way way too little else.

This isn't really what

From: ChaseR@eureka.org
To: badadditude@hottmailer.com
Date: 26 November 11:17am
Subject: Forget my last letter

I decided I wasn't going to finish that last letter or even send it, I was so frustrated. But when I started closing down, I accidentally hit the "send now" button instead of that "close window" box, so out it went and I didn't even notice.

I just pulled it from the "sent mail" file and reread it. It started off fine, but then I forgot I was writing you, Jeremy, and just started pounding the keys like it was my journal. I'm totally embarrassed, but I know you'll just pitch the e-mail and won't bring it up again.

So for Thanksgiving dinner, my grandparents were over, and my one aunt who isn't married, and Mallory and her new friend Linda from school whom she invited home since Linda couldn't fly all the way to Seattle for the weekend, and my parents' friends the Germains, who have two sons in college older than Mallory. Dad always improvises the grace, and it was nice enough, but after thanks for our good health and our good company and all, he says this part—I guess he always does—about being thankful for having enough food on the table, and it made me think about Jeff's family. It just made me sad. I felt sorry thinking of them eating deer all the time, or maybe not having enough, and not even having deer for this year because Mr. Randolph sure won't be attracting any deer this year if the urine does what it's supposed to do. Even if

I never went onto the Randolphs' land again, I bet it's too late for this season.

We've got to pack for the weekend, and I've got to bike over to Marylynne's, too, to drop off an assignment she missed. She's getting nicer. I guess her folks are getting along better. Happy Thanksforeverything,

Chase

q : ¬)

P.S. Remember you don't have to write back very much. Just hit the "reply" button and add a few words at the top just so I know you got THIS one.

From: ChaseR@eureka.org
To: bill_weaver@ohdept.wildlife.pickway.net
Date: 26 November 4:52pm
Subject: Another question

Dear Mr. Weaver,

I know it's a holiday and you're probably not retrieving e-mail, but as soon as it's possible, can you tell me how long urine will discourage deer from coming near? How often does it need to be reapplied to stay effective? I've been using human urine if that's important to know.

Thank you for your advice, and Happy Holiday.

Chase Riley

From: ChaseR@eureka.org
To: badadditude@hottmailer.com
Date: 26 November 7:01pm
Subject: <no subject>

Dear Jeremy −Õ∫Ô−

You're right. I was thinking the same thing myself. I don't know if I can just ride over to the Randolphs' and fess up. I thought about finding some corn from some other field (though everything's been plowed under around us) and replacing the stuff I pissed on, but I'm pretty sure, since it's been so dry, that the ground has the scent, too. My method wasn't what you'd call precise. I can't simply tell Jeff and have him tell his dad. Yes, I'd be embarrassed, but it's more than that. No, I wouldn't be afraid of what they'll do. They're not the kind of people who are going to start a feud or something. And I don't believe I could really be arrested for just taking a leak, or even a bunch of them. Perhaps I could be charged with trespassing, and maybe I'd have to pay a fine. (Hell, hunting season is ALL ABOUT trespassing, as far as I can tell!)

On the other hand, if the other property owners discover that I scattered their deer blinds and pried away their steps and did the urine treatments—maybe all together that could be trouble. But you agree with me: I HAD TO DO SOMETHING.

If I were Jeff, I think I'd hate me. Jeff won't understand what I did. Or why. Or that it wasn't personal. It wasn't about him or his family—it was about the deer. But then it turned out to be about his family, and that wasn't in the Big Plan.

Jeremy, you may be the only one who understands the situation. (You do, don't you?) Plus, you understand algebra, and I don't think my tutor will be available come next week.

Tomorrow morning's opening day of the season, and I know Jeff and his dad are both going out. I also learned from Marylynne that Jeff's not really into the killing part as much as the part where he just keeps his dad company and helps. He can probably calculate the trigonometric angle of the fired bullet in relationship to gravity and the earth's curve. Whatever that means. He's really smart.

I did convince my parents that we had to be away (or they decided at the same time that we ought to see my other grandparents in Indianapolis), so we're driving there for the weekend—with the dogs, of course. Mom does get upset when Bonner goes bonkers. (She's nicknamed him Bonkers.) Sister Mallory, home for a total of five days, announced that she does not wish to go, but, too bad! She still has to be the daughter when she's home from college. SORRY.

If we can stop off in Columbus on the way back, I'll call and we'll get together. I want to hear all the new stuff you've been rehearsing. I want to do anything but think about being me.

Chase

P.S. This isn't funny, I know, but I couldn't stop my brain from thinking, What if I end up being an entry in the BEACON's "Police Activity" report? Can you almost picture this?

> >>>>>Beaver Creek, December 1. Police were called to the property of a Farview Hills man who complained that someone had been fouling the area around his deer stand. Upon investigation, police discovered the smell of urine. This was not the first report they had received of this kind. The pee-petrator is still large.

(Knowing our paper, they'd probably spell the word "fowling," like someone had been throwing turkey giblets all over the ground, and then not even noticed the typo in "perpetrator" or the missing "at" before the "large." We have better proofreading in the newspaper club at school.)

Bye again from the I.P. Daily Home for De-leak-quent Boys,

Still Chase

q:¬|

From: ChaseR@eureka.org
To: badadditude@hottmailer.com
Date: 30 November 6:57am
Subject: Home again, back to school

−Û∫Ũ−

GREAT to see you. (Great new glasses, too. See, I changed your smiley.) Not enough of a visit, but still great. Never the less (I've decided this should be three words), I have lots to report since you and I really had no chance to TALK. Everyone sitting in a booth at Big Al's Barbecue wasn't really the best way to spend our one afternoon visit. Sorry!

So starting with the drive Friday at dawn, everything has happened faster than the usual fast. I mean we were all packed in the car (and MnD couldn't bring up the topic then because Mallory's friend Linda came along), and next we entertained my grandparents for two days, and finally we tried to visit nearly everyone we'd ever known in Columbus.

Let me back up. After Thanksgiving dinner I collected e-mail, and there was your reply and one from the county extension guy Bill saying that a "treatment" of urine should last two weeks, unless there's been a good rain. (I guess I knew it was something like that, and we haven't had rain.) But I didn't know what to do. I had to admit I had this sinking, awful, guilty feeling, although I didn't know why. I mean, I feel justified doing what I'd been doing, but now I also feel miserable when I think about Jeff and his family.

But no one else is thinking anything at all, I don't think. Just business as usual. (Or wait, maybe even I don't think, and all my supposed thoughts are just vibrations of some neuro-plasma sitting in a jar on some scientist's shelf.)

Well, I made the mistake of talking to Mallory. THAT WAS THE ONE MISTAKE I REALLY DID MAKE. I hadn't told her I was trashing the neighbors' deer spots. I may have hinted, but she was too busy to pick up on my clues. She hit the ceiling and started shouting at me, which she used to always do, but not since she's been at school. (One nice thing about long-distance.) Coincidentally, Dad was right outside my room in the hallway. I don't know what he heard exactly, but he invited himself in, sat on the bed, and asked, "Is something going on I should know about?" Translation: "Let's have it NOW and I mean it!"

I had to tell him. I guess I wanted to. The whole thing. We still had guests in the house, so Dad listened and nodded, but I could tell he was shocked. (The kind of culture shock kids give parents, I guess.) I'm not the worst kid in the country or even in this county, but he figured me first runner-up for both. "We'll discuss this later, YOUNG MAN." He went back out to the dinner table as if he really thought he might relax over another cup of coffee. He was fuming mad. Mad like when I slammed the car door on Mallory's hand ACCIDENTALLY. Mad like when you and I used his weed whacker and broke the starter thing ACCIDENTALLY.

I do realize it was no accident that I'd been harassing hunters for the last few weeks. ("Harassing," I have now learned, is the lawyer's fancy term for interfering, even though no one knew I was doing any interfering, so I don't see how that's harassing.) Plenty of people—not the neighbors, of course—would have thanked me for doing what I did. I read on the Internet about this one man in Colorado, I think, who was charged with harassing and had to go to court because he was cranking up his boom box as loud as it would go

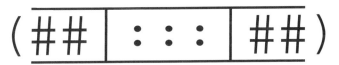

to startle the deer and scatter them out of the hunters' range. (That's a boom box, though it looks like a Band-Aid.) I guess the court case was battled for a long time.

I'm already late for school. More later,

ChaseR

q:¬)

I found one CRIMES OF THE COUNTRYSIDE in the paper this morning as I was scarfing down a muffin:

> >>>>>Hebron, November 22. Police were called by a Timber Ridge woman to the scene of a tornado. When police arrived they could find no tornado and the sun was shining, but they did notice that the woman had been drinking. No further action was required.

From: ChaseR@eureka.org
To: badadditude@hottmailer.com
Date: 30 November 11:07pm
Subject: Re: Re: Home again, back to school

–Û∫Ù–

You are so great. Thanks for the note back. I don't think I'll ever be able to drink iced tea again.

And, no, I never saw the movie or read the book, but I've seen their website. It's got scads of graphics and movie clips you can download. I'll find the address and forward it. And also, I know some kids who hang out in that one teen club chat room, but it's so boring waiting to see the reply from the one person you want to talk to appear on your screen after like twenty replies from other jerks talking about stuffed animals and seeing Ricky Martin's belly button in his video. Marylynne doesn't even watch MTV, which is so unlike everyone else it makes me like her more.

Back to what happened. So after everyone left, my dad goes into this too calm voice that he has and he announces that we (WE means HE + ME), "WE are heading over to the Randolphs' this very instant and, because we will all be away and Bonner will not be affected, you personally are to invite Jeff and his father to hunt our land for the weekend. You made the problem. You make the solution."

I'll skip the next part since that's where I shout at Dad, "@#%$&!!£," using words they NEVER let me get away with, and then Mom tries to change Dad's mind, even though she'd originally agreed that we should go over. Then Dad says: "I'm sorry this has to go against your own beliefs, but, truthfully, Chase, I'm not sure a person your age even HAS actual beliefs; I think your beliefs are still being formed." Then he tells me I've jumped the gun, taking matters into my own hands. JUMPED THE GUN. How about that!

Jeremy, you know my dad. And you know me, too. I couldn't help it: I burst out crying and it took me awhile to stop. It wasn't what he said so much as just looking at our dogs. The two of them were right next to my feet the whole time, and they just made me feel so sad, like they were the only two members of my family I could really trust. More than my parents. More than all those hyperventilating FOR and AGAINST people ranting on the Internet. More than anyone around here. I could trust the dogs and they knew that I could be trusted, and just knowing that was making me cry. (No, I'm not going to draw a smiley of Chase boo-hooing.)

I've been writing too much. And I'm too tired to keep writing. I'll get back to this later. But I have to write it all down and then send it and DELETE THE WHOLE THING—from my brain, not just my computer.

Chase

q¬ Zzzzz

From: ChaseR@eureka.org
To: badadditude@hottmailer.com
Date: 1 December 7:23am
Subject: Re: Re: Re: Home again, back to school

J:

OK, so the story continues after that short break. I swear, I was so tired I couldn't even spell Zzzzz. By the way, my dad forgot to tell me you called—that's why I never called back. Read on for why.

So back to Thursday night, post-Thanksgiving. Mom stayed home and made turkey sandwiches for the next day's road trip. So Dad and I drive over. When we walk in, I see how Dad is looking around and I can tell he's uncomfortable seeing how the Randolphs' house is so crowded and small. We're the closest thing to being their neighbors and our farmhouses were probably built around the same time, but ours had an addition and it's maybe twice the size of theirs, and I'm sure that made Dad feel even worse about why we were there. Like we were the rich people coming to do the poor people a favor. Not that we are rich, really.

So I have to do the talking. Really, I was willing to admit what I'd been doing around the Randolphs' place—but telling the Randolphs to come right on over and hunt our land—that was different. That wasn't right and we've all heard a zillion times how two wrongs don't make a right. Jeff's brothers and sisters hung out in the TV room, and I could hear his mom shoving stuff down the disposal. So I start explaining—just the basic things—and Jeff just stands there, like he's waiting, like for his dad to excuse him from the table. He doesn't say a word. Dad doesn't say a word. Mr. Randolph doesn't say a word. Finally, after I say all the words, Jeff's dad says, "We truly appreciate you two taking the trouble to come and tell us, and we appreciate the offer to hunt your property." Come to find out, they only have this narrow lot between our place and the Osgoods', and that's a real challenge for hunting. Jeff keeps looking at the ground like he doesn't know me. Which is probably true. He had to be embarrassed that this friend of his had been pissing iced tea around their deer stands, day after day. I was so dizzy from everything spinning in my head, I fell asleep in the car on the way home. It's a four-minute drive.

But before dinner last night, Jeff rode over. He came by . . . not to say thanks, exactly, but—what he actually said was they had been lucky and his dad had shot his limit of three deer: one on the morning we left and two on Sunday morning. Jeff said, "We filled our freezer and the other one in the garage, and we even took some over to the church where they feed all these people who are out of work since the ASCO plant closed." He acted like nothing ever happened between us, and I guess nothing really did—between us, I mean. This isn't about him or even his dad. Or even me. Maybe I don't know what it's about. It's about Bonner. And it's about this giant culture shock wave that keeps buzzing through me ever since we arrived. Dad was right. If we lived in Columbus, I'd never have started worrying and dreaming and thinking about all this. But we don't.

Jeff hung around awhile. We watched some wrestling that came on TV. (Turns out one of Jeff's aunts used to be married to a guy who's sometimes on, a wrestler named Psycho, but he wasn't on when we tuned in.) Mom made a big deal of inviting Jeff to dinner. I think she wanted things to be forgiven and forgotten, too. Jeff said maybe next time. He had to drive with his mom to Zanesville to drop off his two stepsisters.

One odd thing (I guess it's not odd, it's more ironic): Bonner loves Jeff. Pirate, as you remember, doesn't love anyone—I mean, he does, he loves everyone, but he doesn't show it. But Bonner sat with Jeff, and Jeff just rubbed and rubbed on that dog's favorite itching places. So then as Jeff's leaving, he says, "By the way, Chase, we didn't end up coming over here to hunt."

I didn't understand what he was saying. "What do you mean?" I said. "I thought you guys shot three deer."

And Jeff says, "We did. But not here. My dad has these friends who'd already invited us to their land near the Hocking Hills. I didn't know that when you were over. Deer down there are so thick, the farmers lost most of their corn this year. Anyway, since you wouldn't have known, being out of town and all, I thought you might want to know."

Jeremy, that blew me away. I couldn't think of what to say. Finally, I asked him, "But how come? We gave you permission to hunt here, and it was my fault—"

"We didn't need to, didn't want to. I get how you feel about

136

hunting. Sometimes I feel a little of what you do, but it's not the way we do things. Not in my family, anyway. So after you left, when I told Dad about your dog being shot and being scared and all, he just said, 'Well, the Rileys sound like good people,' and then he went to get the gear together. That's all the talking we did about it. Next morning, we set off for the Hocking Hills."

You know, Jeff didn't have to tell me any of that. He could have let me believe they hunted here and shot those deer here, and maybe that would have been justice. And maybe knowing they killed those deer right here where I walk Bonner and Pirate would have made a difference in my wanting to hang out more with Jeff. But things didn't happen that way. He changed things. Maybe I didn't, but Jeff did.

When I thanked him for telling me—for telling his dad about Bonner—he just shrugged, like none of this, not anything in the last few days, was going to change a thing.

After Jeff left, my folks and I finally had the Big Talk, but after talking with Jeff, I was already feeling like whatever they'd say wouldn't change anything, either. The fact is, my folks hadn't really acted mad since Thanksgiving night, only that hurt or disappointed routine, which is worse than angry in a way, right? They didn't ask me why I had done those things or what good I thought I was doing. They knew. And they didn't expect me to apologize to any of the other property owners, mostly because we've never met any of them and some of them don't even live here. (You got to admit, it would be pretty stupid to look up their names and phone numbers only to call and introduce ourselves, "HI, WE'RE YOUR NEW BAD NEIGHBORS.") So I'm lucky in that way, if a kid whose dog suffers from some kind of shell shock can still be lucky. I'm lucky like a deer is lucky when it's stuck in a car's headlight beams and doesn't know which way to turn, but then jumps away at the last second.

I know I'm not so lucky barely making good grades in school because of—because of everything I've written you over the last couple months. But you know what else? I don't want to be LUCKY. Lucky is just when something goes better than you thought it would because you didn't do enough to make sure it would go really well. I know I have to do more. I guess I've known that for a while.

That's basically what Mom and Dad wanted to talk about. They didn't even use the word "punishment." "What kinds of changes do you think might improve things?" That's what they said. I think Miss Dummery gave them that line! But it is true that improving things a little at a time may be the only possibility because there's no solving things: every year we live here, it's going to be the same, and this season isn't even over yet. Like I said, what Jeff told me made the first improvement and maybe I can make others follow.

Also in the BOVINE CREEK BACON this morning, since almost half the paper's devoted to hunting, were two top stories: HUNTERS WOUNDED IN MISFIRING and WHITETAIL DEER ABOUND, HUNTERS SAY. The third story should have been: DUH! Those same two headlines have probably been used every year since the paper was founded. The homemaker lady did her column on shepherd's pie made with venison. That wildlife guy I was e-mailing wrote about some other state's new program where they use darts to tranquilize deer and relocate them to less populated places. There's a study being done to see if we could implement something like that in Pickway County, but the program's expensive and takes lots of experts and equipment. So, after we build a public library (all we've got now are a shelf of videotapes at Sweeney's next to the buns and cupcakes), and after we redo all the county gravel roads with asphalt, and after they remodel the post office so there's more than Mrs. Sanders to sell the stamps, and after we build a Playland for the elementary school, and after who knows what else, then we'll raise money for tranquilizer darts. Right.

My parents HELPED ME decide that if I spend only one hour per day on the computer that could "improve things." At least through the rest of the year. (Your being here the week after Christmas will cut down on my e-mail.) I'm also supposed to contribute to some of the bigger farm projects to keep my mind on positive things. (Thanks for the tips, Miss Dummery!)

Me thinking of ten positive things ⇒ ⊕⊕⊕⊕⊕⊕⊕⊕⊕⊕q : ¬ ,

Me going to bed tonight ⇒ ⌐q' ¬)   / ⌐

Me going to bed tonight thinking ⊕ thoughts about Marylynne ⇒ ⌐q' ¬) \ | / ⌐

See you,

Chase

Oh, also this from the EAGER BEAVER BEACON, a choice pair:

CRIMES OF THE COUNTRYSIDE

>>>>>Cliffside, November 24. When police arrived at a Hickory Road residence on a report of a domestic dispute in progress, the woman involved was throwing a headless concrete yard rooster at her husband.

>>>>>Beaver Creek, November 24. A Walnut Hollow woman called police when she couldn't get her son to get dressed for school. [This is NOT me. I wouldn't dream of going naked to school.]

From: ChaseR@eureka.org
To: riley79@kentstate.edu
Date: 1 December 8:11pm
Subject: Hi

Dear Mallorina,

I know it's almost finals week, so you don't have to write back, and since we talked a few days ago, you know everything anyway. MnD are being pretty cool (especially when they're not home). And I have school for two and a half more weeks, so you'll be home before I'm done. (And you can help rewrite my paper for English.) (Well, you can at least give me some advice.)

But really, here's what's on my to-do list since everything happened:

- demolition work with handyman Sid on the barn that's fallen down
- help Dad cut and stack firewood
- strip wallpaper from the hallways (five layers at last count) with Mom
- insulate top floor of garage

This last thing I'm psyched to do for two reasons: I'm moving my bedroom into the top room of the garage. Mom wants us to call it the "carriage house" . . . OK. And I'm soundproofing it. I had this idea at first just to be able to crank up the music. (MnD go to sleep so early and they make me keep my stereo at a whisper.) Awhile ago I met this kid Rocky about five minutes away, who's made this pretty decent recording studio down in his basement. I took my guitar over once and we ran through a few songs. Nothing great, but, you know, we were just getting our bearings. We're supposed to get together again. I guess I was supposed to call him and I will. So like I was saying, Rocky's stuck egg cartons to every wall, and it totally cuts out the outdoor sound.

The main reason to add the extra insulation is Bonner, so when there's gunfire, he can come up there and—well, I hope—he won't hear anything and he'll be calm. MnD have agreed to spring for the supplies and they're being encouraging, though I think right now they'd encourage me if I wanted to start a lemonade stand or do puppet shows for little kids if that would make me forget about deer stands. We'll have to see.

Jeff is helping with some of the construction, too. I think if you were born in Pickway County, you just know carpentry, wiring, how to fix all kinds of machines—tons of stuff. Maybe you just have to learn everything when you're out here sort of on your own. So Dad's hired him to help out on Saturdays.

And I have nothing else to tell you about Marylynne because I don't want MnD to be making a big deal about my having a girl who is a friend, and could become a girlfriend.

Get all A's. I think I'll get one in Spanish, anyway. You're supposed to say: "¡Que bueno, Señor Chase!" 🖐 (high-five)

See you soon!

From: ChaseR@eureka.org
To: badadditude@hottmailer.com
Date: 3 December 5:13pm
Subject: TAKING IT TO THE STREETS!

Jeremy –Û∫Ù–

Guess what? I just signed up for driver's ed next semester! I don't know how I got in, but Miss Dummery just said there was an opening and I'm in. Of course, it's just the classroom part. I won't have my temps yet, but this will be one of my electives starting January. Dad says he was thinking about getting a used pickup truck for the farm—a Tacoma or a Ram. But all that's a ways off and something "to discuss, son, . . . [drum roll!] . . . after some Genuine and Sincere Improvements." Which probably won't be before I'm sixteen anyway.

I don't care what kind of car, as long as it's not a riding lawn mower.

Had to tell you! Later,

Chase

q**8**¬)   (new drag-racing shades)

P.S. Can't wait for your visit!

From: ChaseR@eureka.org
To: riley79@kentstate.edu
Date: 9 December 9:59pm
Subject: Homecoming instruction

Dear Mall,

Don't forget to bring my Living Dangerously CD you, uh-hum, ACCIDENTALLY took. And please, pleez, puh-leeze, don't forget to pick up all the egg cartons you had the cafeteria save. I know it's a lot to cram in your trunk, but that's why you took your car back at Thanksgiving. I know you won't let me and Bonner down. Me begging $\Rightarrow$ $\ q:\neg$PLEEZ!

My new room is starting to look habitable. I refitted some carpeting that used to be in the living room, and for starters, I nailed a whole layer of aluminum and foam insulation panels to the walls. Jeff suggested it. His dad used it on their house. That's cut out a lot of sound—like when Dad's chain-sawing, I can't really hear it except through the windows, and I'm making special panels to plug them up whenever there's thunder or gunfire. It's too dark to leave up all the time.

It's strange keeping Bonner and Pirate up in this room with me. Like we're in a fallout shelter. We've spent the last two nights up here, just to get them used to the space. Part of the strange feeling is that we're up about the same height as a deer stand in a tree, and we're overlooking the forest—at least the part of our forest that starts behind the house. We're seeing what hunters could see while they're waiting. And this morning, when I was up too early again, there was a deer off in the distance, within shooting range, I guess, if I were a hunter and I had a gun. It really is beautiful seeing down on things for a change—the way religions always think of their gods looking down—but beautiful doesn't make me want to grab a gun just so I can keep everything from turning and running from me. I think I'll like living over the garage.

The garage will not be known as the carriage house.

Once the egg cartons are glued on and once I've finished the inserts for the windows and once the music's turned up, we'll be in our own little world, as if that's even possible. But maybe it'll work better than getting more pills for Bonner and whatever else I need. (| : : : |)s maybe. Just a place to chill out during gunfire, thunder, Culture Shock waves.

Sure, I'll go halves with you on whatever you pick out. Just make sure MnD would really like the ornaments as much as YOU really like the glass blower. They won't be blinded by LUV. Besides, I don't have any other great ideas for Christmas. If his stuff really is cool, and you think a girl my age would like it as well, buy one more ornament and I'll pay you back. You'll meet Marylynne when you're home.

Speaking of presents, the dogs are hoping you'll be bringing them more of those organic biscuits you got at the co-op there. The peanut butter were the favorite.

See ya,

q : ¬)

From: ChaseR@eureka.org
To: buddy list #1
Date: 10 December 10:01pm
Subject: Volume I, No. 6 (Way Late Edition)

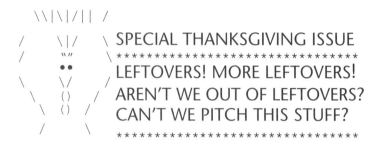

SPECIAL THANKSGIVING ISSUE
****
LEFTOVERS! MORE LEFTOVERS!
AREN'T WE OUT OF LEFTOVERS?
CAN'T WE PITCH THIS STUFF?
****

Hey, everyone. Hope your Turkey Day was great and that you saved room for pie! I've found two new country-style pies I bet you never had: sure, we've got pecan and pumpkin, but how about chess pie, made with chesses—you know, CHESSES! Dee-lish! (I haven't found out what a chess is, either, but the pie is like a meringue thing with some sugary creamy filling where the fruit should be.) Also there's grape pie made by my neighbor Jeff's mom from her own concord grapevines. The pie sounds like it's missing peanut butter, but it's also dee-lish and puckery sweet.

We've had lots to be thankful for this holiday, maybe more than usual, but then maybe everybody feels that way. I can't say that five months into country life convinces me I'm a country boy. Dad's been commuting to work and then working around here most every night and all weekend. Mom's been sort of half commuting. Mallory's at school. I basically hold down the fort with the two dogs. On the other hand,

Bonner and Pirate are absolutely convinced that country life is the greatest thing in the world, and they wonder why they ever had to spend any part of their lives walking city sidewalks on a leash.

I've had the worst algebra teacher in the universe, a Mr. Denton, who calls us by our last names—"Mister Riley, perhaps you'd care to share your answer with the group?" He talks less about math than he does about "Good Citizenship," by which he means not whispering or passing notes in class. But this kid Jeff I know has been helping me, and we've been hanging out more. He plays harmonica better than anyone I've ever heard, not that I can play any songs that have a harmonica part yet. There's also another kid Rocky who's older and who I don't know that well, but he's invited me over to record some in his basement. Over Christmas break. (We'll certainly record "I Saw Mama Kissing Santa Claus"—and 27 other holiday favorites.)

I've only had to see the principal twice, once for "Discourteous Behavior" (thank you, Mr. Denton) and once for this special meeting "to get to know the new kids on the block." (We don't even have a block—that's how "totally in tune with the students" he is.) But I visit the guidance counselor weekly to help with my Adjustment Phase and Academic Craze and Bad Case of Culture Shock. So school's still school.

After school's been my own time, except for newspaper club, which turns out to be the only place where people like that I can type really fast. Otherwise, I have tons of chores and work to do around the farmhouse and the barn. I'm remodeling my own new room above the garage, which is the best part. Anyone need firewood? We're chunking up dead trees by the dozen, and we've stacked a fortress of cords everywhere. Come and get it! Free! Also free: unlimited pinecones and grapevines for holiday craft time. Also free: cartons of Old Mr. Fitzweller's junk that he left here when he died. (I think his first name was "Old" and his middle name was "Mr." because all the people we know call him that.)

Everyone here is just waiting for Christmas break. I guess that's what Thanksgiving signals: Christmas break's around the corner, but first, the long-awaited deer season. That part's been a little hard to stomach. A lot hard. We didn't exactly have deer season back in the city, but really we did, since the deer would have been around where our new development went in. The deer just crowded up around the outskirts. (I just read that we have 40 deer in every square mile. On the average. There used to be ten!) Seventeen years from now, I'm lobbying for cicada season. Get those hunters a real adversary. We've got enough cicadas to feed a family of six (with a deep freezer) for seventeen years. (If you deleted the Cicada Pizza recipe, just e-mail me back.)

Thanks for writing me, everyone. I know I didn't come through with these e-newsletters as I promised, and I did even worse at answering e-mail. (I did worst of all on my essay "Steinbeck's OF MICE AND MEN," even though I know more about < : 3) ~ ~ ~ ~ than Steinbeck ever could have.)

Every day I think a lot about all the stupid stuff we did together in the old school and the old neighborhood. (I know it's not OLD to you, but for me it's forever going to have that extra "old" just like Old Mr. Fitzweller.) Some days I even remember the not-stupid stuff we did, and it makes me miss being there with you. Funny to be home but to feel like you're missing home.

But I have found more Top Ten Reasons to Live in the Country to round out my earlier list:

- ➤ Mr. Sweeney will stock whatever we want at the general store. Mom likes this one kind of root beer, and he orders it just for her.
- ➤ We also had bushels of chestnuts from our own trees. Some we roasted just the way those vendors do in New York City, and they are better than any other nut you'll ever meet. (Except for Doughnut! Are you reading this? How come you never write?)
- ➤ You can mountain bike for hours and never come across the same track.
- ➤ You never have to listen to your neighbors working on their cars or cranking up their TVs while you're concentrating on homework.
- ➤ Taking naked showers outside in the yard, even in the cold. (I know you don't ever take showers with clothes on, it's just that being naked outside is different than inside, so I had to write it.)
- ➤ Oh, and maybe my favorite part of being out here is the sky. The dogs and I go out after dark and lie in the grass, just staring up at the stars. They're the same stars as the ones above Columbus, but without the city glow—and there's no other glow from our own village—I can see them like they never

really existed before. You could count them if you were really desperate for a hobby and you had all the time in the world. All that giant black and all those holes of white make you feel incredibly little, littler than even ants on earth must feel, especially if you remember that all those stars are just more suns, and that every sun could have planets and moons circling them and people on them staring up—or maybe it's down!— at our sun and thinking how tiny and far away WE are. Staring up like that makes everything shrink. So when I come back in the house, I try not to let everything get big again.

Well, readers, I'm here if anyone's driving east for Christmas break. We aren't going anywhere and neither are the stars or the deer or the mice or the raccoons or the spiders . . .

Bye for now from the 90-Acre Nature Preserve, Dog Rehab Center, and Cicada Plantation,

ChaseR

q : ¬)

Of course, we still have time for your favorite and mine:

CRIMES OF THE COUNTRYSIDE

>>>>>Thornview, November 21. Police on patrol near Hamilton Parkway discovered a door standing open on an apparently empty house. When police checked it out, they found the owner inside watching the Weather Channel. No action was required.

>>>>>New Roscoe, November 24. Police on patrol saw several subjects standing ouside Larry's Tavern, yelling and trying to get the officers' attention. One woman explained that a man inside the bar was exposing himself. Police TRIED TO MAKE CONTACT with the man, but he ran. [All I did was put the paper's words in caps. Nothing's > - " , " , " , " - { D > about this story.]

*　　　*　　　*　　　*　　　*　　　*　　　*　　　*　　　*

In our NEXT ISSUE:

> Inexpensive Country Crafts for Christmas (including acorn snow-men!)

> Top Ten Ways to Suck Up to Santa (No, you're never too old to be on Mr. Kringle's good side!)

> And the answer to Today's Quiz Question:

> Q: Who decided that every kid in this world has to read OF MICE AND MEN? Is it really that much better than any other book ever written?

From: ChaseR@eureka.org
To: riley79@kentstate.edu
Date: 11 December 10:33pm
Subject: Re: Re: Homecoming instructions

Whatever you say, but one last thing. Don't worry, you're not supposed to reply to this.

I'm glad you'll be home tomorrow.

I know you don't want your little brother lecturing you, but since you won't be arriving until after dark, and you remember what happened to Mom that night, you have to watch for deer on the roads. You're not used to seeing them. You turn some bend, and one is just standing there looking up at you, kind of amazed that anyone would be out here in what's supposed to be wilderness. As soon as you exit the interstate, be ready to brake, even before you see a deer, because they're right there, running from one thing or another, and maybe from you. Just watch.

Do a bang-up 💣 job on your last paper! Make me and MnD real proud.

Love from the Pickway Township Watchtower and Sincere Improvement Center,

Your Deer Brother

3 : ¬)